Waves

Ten Stories (No Elevator)

John English

©2013 BHSW Inc.
ISBN-13: 978-1492831549
ISBN-10: 1492831549
Pronghorn Publishing, an imprint of BHSW, Inc.
Old City Hall Building
606 6th. Avenue, Belle Fourche SD 57717
Pronghornpublishing.com

Contents

Introduction

My wife found a body in the waves.

This was three years ago. We were visiting family in Kilkee, on the west coast of Ireland. She liked to get up early and do the cliff walk, a three-mile path that follows the shore from the horseshoe beach into neighboring hills, many of which have already fallen into the ocean. Hard black basalt has been fighting the Atlantic there for millennia, and the drop-offs are dramatic. In County Clare, one can stand on the edge of a cliff with the wind in one's face and look down hundreds of feet into the swell, with no guardrail in sight.

She was walking up a slope in the path, the precipice a few feet to her right, when she noticed something bright bobbing in the tide below. It turned out to be a rain jacket on a young German guy, a PhD candidate who had slipped off the Cliffs of Moher up north, two days prior. He was taking photographs at the edge of a 600-foot drop, and he did. The waves had carried him twenty miles and deposited him in a small sheltered cove.

Strangely, the finding didn't affect our holiday too much. There was remoteness to it, perhaps because the poor man was a football field away and thus somehow less personal. My wife didn't do anything silly like sit bolt upright in the middle of the night with a vision of the corpse before her. After teaching high school for several decades, I suppose she is inured to the vacillations of life's little bumps. She once had a student raise his hand in the back row and ask if he could move because somebody in the next classroom was pushing the blade of a long knife through the wall, and it was making him uncomfortable.

I could sit all day on the rocks around Kilkee and watch waves. My father was fond of saying if one looked straight west at the horizon, the very next parish in Ireland was Boston.

All that water, and only a few rocks at the edge to keep us dry. I like to take off my shoes and socks, find a comfortable spot and let the eddies wash my feet. Waves are mesmerizing: they invite the unwary to slip between them. The salt and silt and sediment give the illusion of solidity – it's safe here, you'll have good footing. Come on in. There's a German guy we'd like you to meet...

Our favorite spot in America is dead center. We live in the ancient Black Hills, an hour north of four dead Presidents carved in a granite outcrop that was stolen from the Lakota by George Armstrong Custer.

The nearest waves are three days east or two days west, and every year or two we make the drive to meet them. We have explored the Pacific coast from Santa Cruz to Seattle and are somewhat acquainted with the waves in its small harbors and bays. The Pacific invites only acquaintance: there is no intimacy. Big and powerful, this ocean is masculine, but its muscles ripple below the smooth skin of deceit. In 2011, an earthquake in Japan drowned a man in the Klamath River in northern California. He was standing on a sandbar, taking photographs. A dangerous thing to do near an ocean...

The Atlantic is a woman. Bitchy, witchy, wild and wicked, driven by hormones and heart, she separates Europeans on either shore.

Stand on the cliffs of George's Head at the north end of Kilkee Bay in late November and the waves are fifty feet high and exuberant as they pound through the wind and rain, arms outstretched, gyrating to a rhythmic crash upon the rocks as they spit spray high, high and down onto the springy, hardened grass above. The mermaids here don't sing a song of sirens. The Pacific may sound like Pat Boone, but the Atlantic is all Melissa Etheridge.

"Yes I am."

We visited Pacifica, half an hour south of San Francisco, and spent a week in August living in a hotel room with sliding glass doors that looked over the beach.

Above was the view from our hotel room, but this picture holds a secret. Between our sheets and the sea, in a rut out of sight, Highway 1 carried a steady stream of invisible traffic through our view.

Each afternoon a misty mantle settled on the surrounding hills. The ground is sedimentary – soft sandstone molded by wind and rain more than waves. From low tide to high, the sea barely rises. Surfers in unnecessary wetsuits paddle out a hundred feet on the flat warm pacific water, waiting for weenie waves – pathetic pillows with lacy edges that comfort rather than confront. Then, awkward because there is little momentum, the surfers wobble a few yards standing and, soon losing balance, fail and fall and fold back down into the lazy soup.

A nautical mile or two from the Cliffs of Moher, and six thousand miles east of Pacifica, the beach at Lahinch in County Clare hosts tougher surfers who must wear wetsuits to ward off hypothermia. Here, the waves are constant, one upon the next, rushing to the edge as though they're late again and don't want to hear about it, dammit.

Irish waves run into each other as words in Ulysses, each scrambling to retreat before the next pours eagerly upon it. Once, Leopold Bloom was charged in court for content. Ever since, readers have charged him with obscurity.

Irish writers never say anything simply.

Perhaps that comes from living on an island: a fear of isolation. When they find an audience, they hold onto it as long as they can, although that's not so true of Irish poets. Well, not all of them. Goldsmith once used three thousand three hundred words to tell us that a village was deserted and nothing was happening. Yeats, on the other hand, captured an entire revolution in just five words: "A terrible beauty is born."

While prose flows, poetry is waves. Here is rhythm, a crescendo of syllables breaching on the beach to decorate the fringe of a tide receding.

At other times waves never reach the sand, crashing instead against the hard shins of cliffs, where bodies bob.

And poetry is craft, demanding respect. As a child I watched a man in Galway, not far from the sea, transforming a pile of rubble into a stacked wall that ran along the boundaries of his field. The rocks lay one atop the next, large ones kept in place by smaller stones, the way blue jays herd a hawk. It shouldn't work, but it has for centuries. Miles on miles of walls walk through the Irish countryside with not an ounce of mortar in them. In America, we tend to build fences rather than walls. They go up more quickly and they don't last as long, but it's easier to talk to your neighbor through a fence.

They come down quicker, too.

My father was a lovely, warm-hearted, decent, generous, welcoming Irishman and a racial bigot all his life. Four score and seven years he lived in a population that was 97% Catholic and 100% white. He never knew minorities, but he knew them well. They understood how to build a wall in those days.

Which is surprising, because talk is the very lifeblood of the island. Well, words are, anyway. There are as many people in Denver as there are in Ireland, but there are far more writers in Ireland.

Bram Stoker, James Joyce, Tom Kinsella, Jonathon Swift, Oscar Wilde, Frank McCourt, Liam O'Flaherty, Sam Beckett, George Russell, Brendan

Behan, George Bernard Shaw, John Millington
Synge, Patrick Kavanagh, Seamus Heaney, Sean
O'Casey, William Butler Yeats, Goldsmith, Oliver
St. John Gogarty, Sean O'Faolain, Flann O'Brien,
Edna O'Brien (a woman, no less!), Brian Friel,
Frank O'Connor, Liam O'Flaherty, C.S. Lewis,
Roddy Doyle…

There is no tide in Denver.

And nowhere in Ireland is more than an hour
from the waves.

Just saying…

So anyway, this body that my wife found:

Another woman on the cliff walk had a
cellphone and she called the police. Two emergency
vehicles rushed along paved cattle trails through the
rock walls, and a boat was dispatched from Kilkee.
Men on top of the cliff used radios to guide the
recovery, and by now the edge had attracted quite a
crowd. Knowing nothing of this, I blithely hopped
in the rental car and drove to the rendezvous point
where I was supposed to meet my wife, only to find
the wide spot in the road filled with first responders.
Somebody said something about a body in the
water, and how it must have fallen off the cliff, and
heart pounding I raced along the path, cold fear
pumping adrenaline as snippets on the breeze
mentioned that the deceased was a tourist.

When I found her, the waves were still doing their thing below, oblivious to our small drama and only mildly annoyed that the recovery boat had taken their prize.

Now when I sit on the edge of the rocks with feet a-dangle in the tide, I look at the sea in a different way. I think less of the distance to the next parish, and more of the countless souls that she has claimed between here and there.

Blood-drained faces floating in the surf.

Titanic was built in Ireland.

All those writers, and most of them spent a lifetime describing the anguish of living on a rock battered by bitchy brine. Words that ring and

wrench and wrap depression in a Sunday suit,
building walls that hopefully each new generation
will stand upon, and not behind.

A terrible beauty is born.

~

Mineral Rights

He was waiting outside the office when I got there, leaning on the fender of an ancient pickup. A Stetson's brim shaded his eyes from the June morning light. When he shoved himself off the truck, I knew he was a wrangler. His walk said time in the saddle.

Jenny wasn't usually late to the office. I'd become so comfortable with her habits that I no longer carried a key to the front door. Unable to enter, I turned and faced him.

"Can I help you, sir?"

"I'd like a quiet word, if I could, Chief."

Up close, he was pale.

"Parole?"

His head lifted a hair and he wiped a nervous hand across his chin. Six one, I thought. Maybe one-seventy.

"Not quite." He smiled, a gentle grin. "Close, though."

Every now and then we'd have one stop in town. They seemed to need a few days to find themselves, to trust freedom, before they went back to whatever sorry habits had landed them in Rawlins. Behind him, Jenny turned the corner with a white donut box in her hands.

"Morning, Chief," she smiled, as she sailed through the unlocked door.

His name was Robert Lane. Thirty-eight months of a five-year stretch for manslaughter, and he'd been released the night before. I was curious about the truck. New parolees don't often have wheels.

He had a job lined up at the B-Bar-BB, sixteen miles north of town. Just wanted to check in and let me know that he was around, before I heard any rumors. I offered him a donut and a cup of black coffee. Then I asked about the conviction, to see if he'd own it.

He nodded. Guilty as charged.

He'd had his own spread in the hills south of Douglas, rough country with scrub cedars and gumbo, but the grass wasn't bad in the spring. He'd run some Angus, eaten antelope and worked on an irrigation system. The place had come with ancient water rights and a dilapidated ditch. The cabin kept out rain and little else, but he liked the solitude.

Five years back, a white one-ton with duallies and a welding outfit had shown up in his yard. Two guys wearing hardhats walked onto his porch. One was round and short, the other big. They hadn't seen him out behind the shed, working a colt in the round pen, so they pounded on the door. The big one turned to spit, an ugly wad of chew packed behind his lower lip, and he noticed movement. By the time they reached the pen, Lane had tied up the colt and was coming to meet them. The logo on the truck door said MidWyo Exploration.

Turns out that Lane didn't own the mineral rights on his place, which was a surprise to him. They wanted to drill a couple of wells, to see what was down there. All across Wyoming, tall derricks were popping up as the state discovered new wealth in natural gas. The high prairie twinkled at night with lights from towers that were visible for miles.

"Call for you, Chief," Jenny yelled from the front office.

Edgar McBain had a grass fire. I was about to excuse myself and suggest that Mr. Lane and I should meet later to continue our chat, when he surprised me. Reaching for his Stetson, he unfolded gracefully from the chair and looked down at me across the gray steel desk.

"Want some help? That's my new ranch…"

Technically, it wasn't a grass fire. There wasn't any grass. The McBain place occupied a gently sloping bench in the eastern foothills and most of the vegetation was stringy sage and low cactus. A couple of creeks ran through it, erratic scars that hopefully would contain the fire. They were running low this June, the seventh year of our drought. Al Harney claimed that it was a meager snow pack higher up, due to global warming. But he was a liberal college professor, and every rancher knew that water came in cycles.

Two red fire trucks pulled off the highway ahead of us as we crested the last rise and saw smoke in the distance. One was from Wheatland. I recognized the yellow hose reel. The other might be Douglas, but I couldn't see how they would have covered the distance so quickly.

We followed them down McBain's gravel road, through a lodgepole arch that announced the ranch entrance, over a cattle guard, and then bumped across a well-grazed pasture littered with prairie dog burrows. With almost no wind, unusual for this country, the fire was crawling slowly in all directions. It only covered two, maybe three acres and the fire crews didn't seem too excited.

We grabbed a couple of shovels from the back of the Explorer and walked forward to the first engine. The strategy was to form two lines, one east and one west, and let the creeks contain it north and south. Robert Lane and I were sent west, where we joined the entire McBain clan shoveling dirt on the leading edge, and furiously pulling sage and Russian thistle with a rope tied to an ATV. In a couple of months the thistles would become tumbling tumbleweeds, but now they were nothing but fuel with roots.

Around noon, the job was done. Ella McBain invited everyone to the house for lunch, but I needed to get back. With Barney in Cheyenne for a trial all day, I was the only law enforcement for almost half a county. Out here, that added up to four thousand souls and a million acres. Robert Lane begged a ride as his truck was still in town.

After checking in at the office, we stopped by Belle's Buffet for a burger. The noon rush was over and a herd of overweight ranchers had already ambled back to their pickups. Retired but not admitting it, they drove errands for their sons, blocked gravel roads to talk about the thirties, occasionally fixed a gap in a fence. We sat up front and I watched through the plate glass of the diner as five drivers in a row rolled through the only stop sign in town. Lunch was on the county, by way of a thank you. I knew we owed him more.

"When do you start at the B-Bar-BB?" I asked.

"Tomorrow."

There was grit on his face, but rolled up sleeves exposed the bleached arms of a man who hadn't seen the sun for a long time.

"The foreman up there is an old friend," he said. "We were in the Gulf together."

Maybe we owed him a lot more.

On the street, a couple of middle school kids walked by with wires in their ears.

"Tell me about the manslaughter," I said.

Visits from MidWyo had become frequent. They set telegraph poles across his pasture and ran power lines. They graded a dirt road through the middle of the property and brought in two drilling rigs. At night, without the benefit of a television, Lane sat on his porch and watched them work, his quiet valley reverberating to the hum of diesel generators. The beef began to lose weight, and his horses couldn't sleep. He had tried to challenge it in court but the deed gave them all the rights they needed to turn his world upside down. As the weeks rolled by, he grew more agitated. Two months in, he loaded up the steers and sold them to an outfit north of Laramie.

As the last cattle truck pulled out of the yard, Lane collapsed in his old leather chair with a beer, emotionally and physically drained. About three minutes later, MidWyo's white one-ton drove up to the house. This time around, the big guy was alone. It was getting dark and he left the truck running, lights trained on the living room window. The house lit up like a football stadium. It hurt Lane's eyes and added to his irritation.

Out on the porch, the MidWyo man stood on the bottom step.

"We had a little accident," he said. "One of your horses."

"What about my horse?"

"Truck backed over him."

"How the hell could a truck back over a horse?"

"Well, he was in the way and one of the guys caught him and tied him to some pipe. Guess we forgot he was there."

Lane felt fury rise, but he was still in control. He followed the MidWyo man across the pasture toward the carnival of lights. At the edge of the site where shadows still played, a group of hardhats stood in a circle. On the ground, Lane's sorrel mare twitched, her head on the dirt, exhausted. Her belly was split wide and her internal organs flowed through the wound. Beyond panic, her eyes locked on him as he bent over her.

"Does anyone have a gun?" he asked.

"Not allowed," one of the roughnecks said. "Company policy."

"We could back the rig over him," a young voice ventured.

"Him? She's a mare." It was all he could say.

"She's a mess," someone in the crowd muttered.

He stood up, trying to remember if the .45 was in the truck or the house.

"We could use this," he heard, and then there was a sickening thud. He turned in time to see the big guy raise a piece of two-inch pipe for a second blow.

A gravel truck went down Main, shaking the diner window as it passed.

It was two weeks before I had any business up north. I had to stop at the Jennings ranch and explain fences to a guy from Pennsylvania. Seems he had purchased one of several new ten-acre "ranchettes" that bordered Bob Jennings' hayfield, and had discovered that the fence line didn't quite match the boundaries on his survey. That fence had been in the same position for a hundred and twenty years and it ran eight miles in a straight line, marking the edge of the ranch. The Easterner, who had just taken early retirement from managing a mutual fund, wanted to move one end of his 660 feet about nine inches to the west. We met at the fence and Bob spent the entire conversation just shaking his head. Never said a single word.

From there I could see the roof of the barn at the B-Bar-BB, tucked in a fold at the base of the hills, sheltering from the wind. On an impulse, I decided to stop by. Robert Lane walked out of the house as I drove up, a toothpick suggesting that lunch had been good. Three other wranglers followed him and they headed toward a round pen tucked up against the leeward side of the barn. We shook hands, and I was glad to see some color in his face. He was relaxed, looked at home.

"Checking on me, Chief?" he smiled.

"Just wondered if you'd like to join us for dinner this evening," I said, the thought forming just in time to give it voice. "Becky makes a mean pot roast." I hoped there was enough left.

He showed me around for a few minutes. The bunkhouse was a double-wide that the family had once used, and the ranch had supplied a decent mount, ropes, gloves, tack and everything he needed to do the job. He rode herd on eight hundred cow calf pairs, fixed fence, worked the ditches and stock ponds, fixed more fence and occasionally drove a tractor. The B-Bar-BB grew most of its own feed, but the wranglers usually didn't get too involved with that end of the business. Robert had been too late for the spring branding, but he was getting ready to help drive a herd up to summer pasture in the mountains, and the prospect was attractive. I envied the simplicity of his life.

When he had wrenched the pipe from the MidWyo man to vent his fury, he had unintentionally opted out. The judge believed him when he said that he'd had no murderous intent, but the roughneck had backed away and fallen forty feet onto a concrete pad. It took him three days to die.

A year into Robert's sentence, MidWyo had taken the ranch as compensation in a civil suit.

With no family or roots, he had now become the quintessential cowboy, owning nothing more than a saddle, an aging pickup and a pretty serious collection of Zane Grays. He had over eighty titles, rescued from his cabin by a friend just days before a vengeful crew of MidWyo roughnecks burned it to the ground. Those, and a couple of photos, were all that remained of his former life.

The saddle was custom. He'd had the horn replaced with a wider Mexican version that was easier to dally round, and the back rose high to support a painful disk that he'd lived with since high school rodeos. Other than that, there was no tooling, except a couple of barely visible swirls embroidered into the fabric seat. It was designed for work, not show, and in this it resembled its owner.

At seven on the nose, there was a knock on our door. Becky removed a red apple pie apron, hung it on a magnetic hook on the fridge and ran her hands through her hair. She gets a little nervous around new people.

I opened the door.

Despite living on a ranch and eating almost nothing but beef, Robert seemed to thoroughly enjoy the leftover roast. Being a cop, I couldn't help notice that he wore a brand new pair of Cinch jeans. I knew this because there was a sticker with a red price tag still stapled to the back pocket. They call me Sherlock down at the office.

I appreciated the effort that he had made.

Becky warmed to him immediately and by the time he left I had the distinct impression that she wanted to adopt him. It was past midnight, so we dropped the dessert dishes in the sink, let the dog back in and climbed wearily to our bed.

It was the first time we'd ever had a convicted felon over for dinner. I thought it went well.

The following Thursday we had a three-inch rain and the gumbo turned to glue. I walked two car lengths from my vehicle to close a swinging gate and my boots got three inches taller. Wet gumbo is as slick as ice but soft, and a truck that was raising dust in fourth gear yesterday might sink to its axles today just being parked on the same dirt road.

I knew I shouldn't have parked there.

I called Jenny at the office and when she quit laughing she tracked down Cyrus Bean at the parts store and told him I needed a tow. He thought it was pretty funny, too. He was two hours out, so I tried the B-Bar-BB to see if somebody might come out with a tractor.

Ella near bust a gut, but she eventually composed herself enough to say that the only man available was the new guy, Robert Lane. She wasn't sure he knew the country well enough to find me, but she'd ask him anyway. She told me not to go anywhere and I could still hear her laughing after I hung up.

Not fifteen minutes later, a lone rider appeared on the road from the ranch on the ugliest Appaloosa gelding I had ever seen. It looked like it had been run halfway through a carwash after losing a mudwrestling match. The front end was a dun, listless brown and from the withers back it was dirty white. The head was huge, the legs short and most of the mane was missing.

Robert never left his saddle – he just flicked his rope and caught the trailer ball. Then he told me to put her in reverse, dallied around the saddlehorn and within seconds the truck was off the soft shoulder and sitting high on the crown of the road.

I made some lame joke about my having two hundred and ninety horsepower and he only had one, and he was polite enough to smile.

Ella may have had her fun with me, but she was a thoughtful woman and she had sent along some sandwiches and iced tea. We sat in the Explorer and ate. Robert said something mundane about the light breeze and how the ground might dry when the sun came out.

I asked him about Rawlins. He'd had four cellmates in thirty-eight months, a job in the kitchen and he walked out a free man. I hadn't earned any more than that, so we talked about horses and saddles and Edgar McBain's gout. As he reached for the door handle, I passed along the rumor that I'd heard over waffles at the diner.

The B-Bar-BB had sold some drilling leases to MidWyo Exploration. He nodded. The McBains had already mentioned it.

I spent most of the next two weeks in court because some dumbass cowboy got drunk a couple of months back and drove his truck through the front window of his girlfriend's house. Well, the house belonged to her husband too, and that had kind of complicated the case, because he shot the cowboy. Twice, but he lived.

I didn't see Robert again until the Labor Day rodeo. Becky and I were in the stands watching bareback and we were both surprised when Bill Henning, the announcer, called his name. We hadn't looked at the program yet, but there he was.

The horse he had drawn was Midnight Visit, so named because the rodeo contractor had woken up one night to find the mare staring through his bedroom window. She had climbed six steps to his deck, and they had a hell of a time trying to get her to go back down.

When the gate opened I thought for just a second that he had missed his mark, but the right-side judge didn't notice anything and Robert stayed on board for the full eight seconds. At the buzzer, his fluid body slid off the bronc and found him a seat behind the pickup man. It seemed so completely effortless, and I envied his athleticism. He slipped to the ground and as he walked back to the chutes, Henning announced that Robert Lane of the B-Bar-BB had scored 79 points, which currently put him in second place.

I made my way around the outside of the arena and nodded to the kid guarding the gate by the chutes. He didn't want to let me in because the dress code called for a cowboy hat. I showed him a badge instead.

I climbed up on the platform and found Robert helping another cowboy tighten the cinch on his riggin. The kid was about eighteen and looked wide-eyed scared. The bronc snorted and shifted beneath him in the chute and the kid raised his feet above the bars to avoid being crushed. His chaps were store-bought new and his hat sported an awfully pretty band that had definitely been added by some girl. (That's my trained eye for detail.)

When they pulled the gate, the kid double-grabbed on the second jump and was disqualified. His face flooded with relief. No re-ride today.

Robert saw it too, and smiled.

At the hamburger stand, two roughnecks in MidWyo jackets were drinking beer and ogling the barrel riders. Several of the ranch hands were sitting at a picnic table watching them, and talking quietly to each other. I sat down at the table, nodded to a couple of the older hands, and suggested that they go watch the saddlebroncs that were just starting. The roughnecks never knew how close they came to visiting the inside of a horse trailer.

About halfway through my second burger, the McBain's granddaughter stopped at the concession stand. Julie was in her first year at Casper College and she had carried a flag in the opening ceremony. As she turned to leave the counter, one of the roughnecks blocked her way. Before he said a single word, he was sitting on the grass looking startled, blood pouring out of his left nostril. I hadn't even seen Robert move, but now he put an arm around Julie's shoulders and walked her over to her grandmother in the stands.

When the second oilman started to follow them, I flashed my badge again. It was the least I could do.

"That was assault," the MidWyo man said. "Ain't you gonna arrest him?"

He pointed at Robert, whose contestant number 602 still flapped on his back.

"Actually, it was battery. What your pal here did was assault. And as the battery was in self-defense, it was perfectly legal."

"Self-defense?" the one with the nosebleed asked. "I didn't even see him. I sure didn't bother him none."

"No, son, but you did frighten the young lady and that was assault. Now, we can continue this conversation in my office, or you two boys can do the smart thing here and head back to the campground."

I was guessing, but most of the itinerant workers stayed in the city campground when they came in from the rigs, using RVs that MidWyo owned.

"Guess you gotta be from here to get some law," Rudolph mumbled. But he picked up his baseball cap and the two of them headed toward the parking lot.

The only thing I can figure is that they saw the rodeo results in the paper that next Wednesday, and connected number 602 to Robert Lane and the B-Bar-BB. By the time I got to the ranch, the main barn was gone. Ella was sitting on a square bale, the flames flickering in her glasses. Her shoulders were slumped and she didn't want to talk.

They did get the horses out, and the only real loss beyond the building was some hay, a little tack and a 1951 Farmall H that had belonged to Edgar's Dad.

The fire had been started at the northeast corner, farthest from the house and the bunkhouse. I found the fire chief and we spent some time looking, but there wasn't much to see. They had used gasoline, but there were no distinguishable tire tracks, no witnesses and no fingerprints. The only thing we had was a possible motive, and a couple of suspects. I could start with that.

A few minutes after nine the following morning, Ella called. Robert Lane hadn't shown up for work, his truck was gone and his kit was missing from the bunkhouse. The crew had all been going through the barn in case there was anything left to salvage, so nobody noticed when he missed morning chores.

He could have been gone for hours.

I asked if the ugly Appy was still in the corral. She walked over to the window to look. The horse was gone, and so was an old two-horse trailer. I thought I might know where.

I found the truck on a gravel road about ten miles south of Douglas, still hitched to the trailer. Standing on the roof I scanned the horizon and found what I thought would be there – the top of a gas well peeping over a ridge. It took almost an hour to work my way through the hills – I had to turn back twice because the Explorer couldn't handle streams – and the sun was beginning to set by the time I got to the well. By then, it was easy to spot, lit up like a 200-foot Christmas tree all painted white, except for a red band at the top where beacons warned low-flying aircraft. All up and down the scaffold, sodium lights glowed brightly.

At the base were a couple of trailers and several MidWyo pickups. I parked in front of a small trailer that looked like a field office. The man at the desk was about sixty with a bit of a spread. He wore a safety vest and his hardhat lay on the desk beside an open laptop. A nameplate said Tony, no last name. He looked me over, eyes resting on the municipal logo on my shirt pocket.

"You're a police chief?" he asked.

"Yup. Looking for a fella named Robert Lane."

"Bit out of your jurisdiction, aren't you?"

"I followed him here. Well, to a spot up the road where he left his vehicle."

"That the guy who used to own this spread?"

I was used to being the one who asked questions, but Tony was used to riding herd on a bunch of wildcats and I didn't think he'd scare easy.

"That's him," I said resignedly. "He had a bit of a run-in with a couple of your boys at a rodeo on Labor Day, and last night his employer's barn was burned to the ground."

"He did time for murder, didn't he? I'm surprised he's out."

"No, not murder. Manslaughter. He was released in June."

"You figure he's looking for my boys?"

"I don't know. Maybe. Or maybe he just needed to get away for a while and this was once home for him."

"We don't allow firearms on the place."

"I'm sorry..."

"If he's armed, we'll need to call the local law. We don't have anything here to shoot back with."

I looked around and found a chair. It had never occurred to me that Robert would be carrying. He didn't seem the type. And then I remembered that he had mentioned the Gulf, and a chill ran up my spine. I really was a lousy detective. My strength was in reading people, not evidence.

"Light's fading," Tony said.

I looked out the window and the western horizon had turned purple and blue in that peculiar way that it does here, a mile above sea level. Close to, the well site was lit like a football stadium. Tony reached for a phone.

"I'd prefer if you didn't," I said. He hesitated, and then put his feet on the desk.

"Talk to me," he said.

Sitting in the Explorer under the bright lights, I waited for him to ride in, truly thinking he would. Somewhere around eleven, I fell asleep. Car doors slamming woke me and it was already dawn, that milky hour before the fall sky warms to full light. The gas well lamps were all turned off, which seemed strange. Men were shouting, and Tony was standing on the office steps, looking up at the well. The two men hanging from ropes there heard none of it.

My strength was in not reading people.

They found him a couple of days later with a self-inflicted wound and no note, no explanation, no apology. It was hardest on Julie McBain, who had not asked him to intervene.

That November, I handed in my badge. Becky and I moved west to the ocean, where I teach Psych at a small community college and spend my days off watching the waves and fishing, often without bait.

My heart just isn't in it.

~

(First published in the Belle Fourche Writers 2013 Anthology.)

Short Circuit

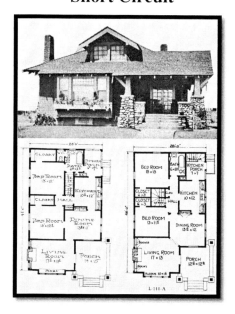

Energy Law II had been in effect for eleven years and Billy Kimble was getting rich. He was even thinking of building a new home, which his inner circle thought was hilarious.

The law had been passed as a result of soaring natural gas prices. It was very simple. New buildings had to present a long south wall to the sun and most of the windows had to be in that wall. Not all plots were the right shape, and that's where Billy came in. As the building inspector, it was up to him to decide whether a homeowner was granted a variance.

His opinion was open to inducement.

The first Energy Law had been designed for automobiles. A senator from Minnesota had proposed the novel idea that speed limits should be tied to consumption. Anywhere there was more than one lane, vehicles with lousy mileage had to stay right, where the limit was thirty miles an hour slower. Oil producing states and the folks in Detroit were up in arms, but most of the country liked the idea. Small vehicle sales soared, while SUVs stood idle.

Initially, commercial trucks were exempt. But by the third year, even the military were included. That was when it finally dawned on members of both houses that conservation was actually popular. So, during an especially hot and humid summer, Energy Law II was passed to regulate the building code.

Everyone in City Hall affectionately called it Billy's Bill.

As with most new legislation, Energy Law II endured numerous challenges in the courts. A man from Delaware wanted to put an addition on his home and contended that he was grandfathered in, since he had owned the home before the law passed. A couple in Phoenix claimed that design restrictions were violating their right to freedom of expression. And an artist in Colorado told a judge that he wanted to look west at the Rocky Mountains, and not at his neighbors to the south. Almost everyone who protested received a variance.

But as the years rolled by and the law became less controversial, there was a marked decline in the number being granted.

In most communities.

The number actually went up in Madison, where Billy Kimble was king.

This was Monday and Billy was at the courthouse early, as usual. Corrupt but efficient was his mantra. At the Flying Duck one night, between a shot and a chaser, he thought about having that translated into Latin and worked into a coat of arms.

A manila folder and a rolled-up set of blueprints lay on his desk, alongside a cup of steaming black coffee. Arlene, his secretary, only ever gave him one job at a time and always had the next one waiting in the wings. The current folder contained a variance request from a man named

Manuel Orantes who wanted to build a new home in the Eastgate subdivision, just outside the city limits. He was still in the county, so Billy had jurisdiction. Manuel's lot measured 300 feet north to south, but was only 50 feet wide. He wanted to orient the house at ninety degrees to the law.

This was exactly the kind of situation that caused Billy Kimble to drool. The guy had already purchased the site, and he owned an older house that he wanted to move in. He wasn't going to walk away, even if the variance was expensive.

He met Manuel Orantes for lunch at the Flying Duck. The guy was punctual, which surprised Billy. Most showed up early, nervous.

They sat in a corner booth where they had enough space to unroll blueprints. Orantes turned out to be short, trim, well manicured and dressed in a decent suit and a slim burgundy tie. Billy wore one of the blue shirts supplied by the city, with his name and job title embroidered on the front underneath the official seal. He was a good fifty pounds overweight and the shirts always felt too tight under his arms, but they were free.

These things always started out the same way. Billy would flat out deny the variance, citing a dozen great reasons why it couldn't be done. Then he's leave the door open about a quarter of an inch, hinting that the only possibility was an extenuating circumstance, which obviously didn't apply in this case. Sometimes they were too dumb to nibble at the bait, rolling up their plans and walking away. He always let them go. He figured those ones were too stupid to keep their mouths shut, too.

Most, like Orantes, asked the question.

"What kind of extenuating circumstances?"

"Well, hardship cases," Billy replied, trying to keep the boredom out of his voice. When you've had the same conversation a hundred times, it was difficult to keep it fresh.

"For example…"

"Oh, I don't know. We had one case where an older couple had lived in their home for almost sixty years and the city needed to move it to extend a school parking lot. The only other site in the neighborhood was the wrong shape. We had to work with that to keep them close to their friends and neighbors."

Orantes shook his head.

"I've never even lived in the house I want to move."

"Well, another time there was a guy who had fought in Korea and 'Nam. He needed to be near the Vet's hospital, so his son bought a site over on North Avenue. The layout wouldn't work for a wheelchair ramp. This guy was about nine hundred years old, so we had to grant a variance and let him build north/south instead of east/west. Turns out, he croaked two weeks after he moved in. Figures, don't it?"

"I'm a Vet, but I don't need access to medical care. Surely there must be some way to make this happen?" Orantes stirred his coffee and stared past the building inspector.

"Jessica and I have already purchased the house. We've always loved it. One of those Sears bungalows, you know? Big old porch out front, divided lites, the works. Been driving by there for years and when it finally went up for sale, we found out that it had to be moved. That's where they're going to build the new Federal Building. We've lived in Eastgate since we got married and this lot is the only undeveloped one left out there. Plus, it's only half a block from our house."

Orantes took a swig of coffee and stared earnestly at the inspector.

"The kids wouldn't even have to change schools", he said. "The only reason the lot hasn't sold is that it's the wrong shape for this damn sunshine law."

Billy used his compassionate look. It was one he actually practiced in the mirror. Not all the time, just when he was straightening a tie or something. He'd always known that it was important to seem sincere.

"There is one way, I suppose." He let it float out there, until the words dissipated. Orantes stopped stirring.

"Yeah?"

"Well, we might be able to do something with the minority thing."

"The what?"

"Affirmative action. You being a minority, we might find something to work with there…"

Orantes stared at him with complete incredulity.

"I'm not using my race to circumvent the law!"

There was an edge to his voice. Somewhere in the back of Billy's mind, a tiny alarm began to sound. It was the phrase. Normal people didn't say "circumvent the law". It was something you heard from cops. And lawyers.

"Fair enough," Billy said. "I didn't mean nothing. Just trying to help, is all."

He rolled up the plans, looked at the check and dropped a five on the table. "Well, maybe you can find another lot. Good luck with that."

"Hold on a minute."

Orantes sounded flustered. Billy stopped, stared at Orantes for a few seconds and sat back down in the booth.

"Well?"

"I won't use race, but maybe there's another way to do this."

Billy's antennae were buzzing now. He had never had an applicant actually make the suggestion. It was always a matter of leading them there. He knew before he heard it what Orantes would say next, and he also knew how he must respond. This guy was clumsy, but he had definitely been sent.

"Such as?" Billy asked.

"Perhaps I can help with the cost of the application?"

"How?"

"Is there some fund I can contribute to? Or some fees I can pay that will help the case move forward?"

There it was again. Help the case move forward. Courthouse lingo. Billy was sure now.

"Okay," he said. "You've got my attention. Gimme a minute to use the bathroom, and we'll talk. The coffee, you know? Prostate. I'll be back in a minute."

Orantes nodded.

As soon as Billy was out of sight, he dialed Jim Sorenson on his cell phone. For once, the police chief was in.

"What's up, Billy?"

"Got some guy here to wants to buy a variance, Jim. What should I do?"

"What do you mean, buy a variance? Did he actually offer to pay for one?"

"As good as. I'm at the Flying Duck. In the john. When I go back out there, he's going to make me an offer."

"You sure?"

"Pretty much."

"Okay, Billy. Keep him talking for a few minutes. Give me time to get a directional mike on him. Ten minutes at least. Can you do that?"

"Yeah, we can talk about his house plans, I guess. Just hurry, okay?"

"I'm on it."

Orantes seemed very eager to get down to numbers when Billy returned to the booth. Instead, Billy explained in great detail the prostate problem he was having. When he had gone as far as he could in that direction, he switched to the house plans.

"Are there any other code issues with this house you're moving in?" he asked.

"Like what?" Orantes was becoming a little annoyed.

"Well, it'll be treated like a new building, so the wiring, firewalls, plumbing, insulation, all that stuff will have to meet code."

He got a good four or five minutes out of that, which should have been enough for Sorenson to be in place. Billy rolled up the blueprints and spread his hands on the tabletop. He leaned back, looked in every direction and saw Sorenson in a booth by the door, then leaned forward conspiratorially toward Orantes.

"So, on this fee you mentioned…"

Jim Sorenson recorded the entire conversation. And, just as Billy had suspected, so did the Feds. He asked Sorenson for a copy of the tape and the chief saw no reason not to give him one. By the time the Feds dropped by his office the following morning, Billy's copy had already found a new home at the newspaper. He showed them his fresh, unfolded copy of the Madison Reader, with a photo of Manuel Orantes below a headline that read "Federal Employee Tries To Bribe Building Inspector".

For the next few months, Billy's revenue stream became a trickle. He took it philosophically: just one more cost of doing business. It would pick up again, soon enough. He was right.

That fall, Congress passed Energy Law III, which was an attempt to mandate conservation in a hundred new and different ways. The last of the incandescent bulbs became illegal, gasoline got more additives, and there were even fines for driving with low tire pressure on federal highways. The amount of insulation on refrigerators was increased while their size was reduced. Private water well pumps had to be fitted with their own solar panels. The government was going to buy all vehicles over seven years old except antiques, and recycle them.

Billy paid attention and bought stock in a small supplier for G.E. By the end of the year, the new light bulbs were bringing in more revenue than variances ever had. He plowed the cash into solar panels and wrote new city regulations that required homeowners to convert their wells, and buy only the type of panels his brother-in-law stocked.

By the following summer, Billy had enough in the bank to build his dream home for cash. He purchased an exceptional (and incredibly expensive) site on the edge of the Little Soo, a federal waterway with limited access and only two other homes within a mile or so. He spent some very serious money having plans drawn by a noted architect, and another huge sum paving a half-mile road to the site. He had to sell the G.E. stock to cover the cost, but the panels were still moving like hotcakes, so he wasn't too worried.

On a bright, crisp fall morning he tucked his plans under his arm and walked the three blocks from his office to the Federal Building, to get final approval before breaking ground the following morning. It was just a formality. All of the details had already been worked out with Mel Adams, the Regional Supervisor. Mel had retired in August and his replacement just needed to sign off on Billy's plans. Everything had been sent to the new guy and Billy hadn't heard a single objection. He was in compliance on ducks, geese, native vegetation, runoff, the well, septic, even the sub-base for his driveway.

In all his years as an inspector, he had never made anyone work as hard as this to get a permit. The thought passed through his mind that Federal bribes must be a lot bigger than city ones...

A slim, pretty young lady showed Billy into a walnut-lined waiting room. She brought him fresh hot coffee and offered a newspaper. Exactly twelve minutes later, at nine-thirty on the nose, he was shown into the new Regional Supervisor's office. As the door closed behind him, he glanced at the huge leather chair behind the massive oak desk.

Billy's smile froze.

Looking like a kid in a car seat, and wearing a grin as wide as his chair, was the short, groomed figure of Manuel Orantes.

~

Tea with Sally

The funeral was austere. Edwin saw only one other mourner, a young lady. Not even his father's lawyer had shown up. Stanley had court, and would stop at the house later.

There was little the priest could say about his father that the turnout hadn't.

Later that evening, Edwin sat in the large walnut chair in his father's study. After reading the will and oozing some wisdom, the lawyer had left. Sorting through his father's papers, Edwin realized that this was the most intimate he had ever been with the old man. Now, mentally reviewing the day, he felt saddened that the same held true for all the people his father's life had touched. No one got close. Nobody shared the burdens or the joy, not since his mother's passing when Edwin was nine.

He hadn't consciously recalled his mother's image in a long time. Even now, he was a little awed by the mystery of her absence.

Edwin wondered why these two losses affected him so very differently. His mother seemed unreal, yet the memories caused pain. They were of doctors and pharmacy bottles, the smell of antiseptic and people dressed in black standing in the rain. His father, whom he had spoken to recently, cost Edwin little by his passing but a whimsical sadness that nobody had shown up to say goodbye.

The doorbell rang. It was the young lady from the church.

"Edwin." Her tone suggested familiarity. "I hope you don't mind."

"I don't believe we . . ."

"I'm sorry. Silly of me, really. I'm Sally, and I worked with your Dad. Helped him in his research, handled the phone. He wasn't good with people, you know. Can I come in?"

"Of course." He held the door wide and smiled a welcome, glad now of the interruption.

She led him to the kitchen, asked if tea was okay and filled the kettle. Edwin noted her familiarity with the layout of the house.

"I felt a bit down tonight," she said. "I needed to talk to somebody who knew him. Your Dad, Charlie."

Charlie? His father was Charles. The epitome of stagnant decorum, from bowler to wingtips. A dignified, conservative, urbane Charles.

She made tea and served it. She was more at home in this kitchen than Edwin: it crossed his mind that this might also apply to some other rooms in the house.

"Aside from your work" he asked, "how well did you know my father? Charlie."

"We were friends," she said. "Good friends." And then she smiled gently at him and said, "That's all."

He was embarrassed that the question had been so thinly veiled, and yet relieved that subterfuge was unnecessary. Now he felt he could ask this woman a direct question and know that the answer had value.

"How long did you work with him?"

"Two years. Actually, a little over. I took the job a few weeks after he began the last book, the one about tribal and ethnic funeral customs."

"How was he to work for?"

"Oh, Charlie was a private man. He kept his feelings to himself. I would spend weeks researching some obscure burial chant and when I handed him the written report, he would nod politely and put it in his briefcase. It took me months to realize that he did, in fact, care."

"I grew up with him," Edwin said. "I lived alone with him through high school and college. We spent vacations together, and long winter evenings. We ate, drove and did chores together for twenty-two years, and I'm afraid I never did come to that realization. The cold-hearted son of a bitch never cared about anybody or anything except his research, his books and his tenure."

He could tell that she was a little taken aback at his vehemence. And then she smiled, and in doing so shattered his mood.

"What was he working on lately?"

For a second, she hesitated.

"Something a little less empirical. It came out of the tribal book." She topped off the tea cups, sat on a bar stool and collected her thoughts.

"He wanted to speak with your mother."

For a second, Edwin thought she was joking. But she stared at him over the rim of the cup, her elbows on the countertop between them, and her gaze never faltered.

"My mother?"

"Yes. He came across a village in Indonesia where the funeral rites centered on, well, essentially a séance. The more time he spent on it, the more he became convinced that there was merit to it."

"Merit?"

"Yes. The process was a group dynamic with a local shaman playing a nominal leadership role, but in fact the actions were communal."

"My God," Edwin said. "You sound just like him. I used to call this his lecture voice."

She laughed, and Edwin saw something in her eyes that he liked. Merriment, perhaps: some unguarded joy that decried her serious tone.

"Okay," she laughed. "I'll keep it secular."

And that was amusing, too. His father used to say that. A devout Catholic who knew with every shred of his being that the Church was a myth, Charles had always separated science and faith with that simple phrase. His need to belong was stronger than his need to question.

"This tribe," she said. "They seemed to have the ability to communicate with the recently deceased. Or, at least your Dad wanted to believe that."

No, he thought. His old man would never have bought that crap.

"It may have been the urgency," she said. "The worse the cancer got, the more desperate he seemed to settle something. He wasn't afraid of dying, but he was terrified of not completing something before he ran out of time."

"Completing what?"

"I'm not sure, really. Perhaps making amends? Or, given his self-centered nature, maybe he needed... forgiveness?"

"Who? Charlie? He didn't give a whit for anyone's opinion but his own. You think he wanted my dead mother to forgive him for something?"

"I don't know, Edwin. I just know he was scared. And he was spending all of his time poring over the tribal study, looking for corroborative evidence in other cultures."

"Did he find anything?" Edwin almost laughed, but he sensed her mood and caught himself.

"Actually, yes."

"What?"

"He found something. It wasn't what he was looking for, though."

"So, not a cellphone number to the dead?"

She have him a brief annoyed look, and then continued.

"No, he found pretty strong evidence of telepathy. The shaman, it seems, could communicate with other members of the tribe without words."

"You mean, living members?"

"Yes, people in the same room."

"Come on, Sally! Telepathy? Next, you'll say Houdini is still alive."

Now there was pain in her eyes. He stared into his tea, feeling awkward and a little ashamed.

There were small black leaves in the bottom of his cup. He swirled them gently and they rose to the top, all except one. It looked like a vein, cylindrical. It made a feeble effort to rejoin its kin, and then settled back to the bottom of the cup where it lay exhausted. Edwin thought to himself that this tea had travelled from Ceylon, or perhaps India, as a group. Now, it's demise imminent, the slow vein was abandoned. Its ponderous weight kept it apart from the lighter fragments.

"A bit like your father, wouldn't you say?"

"Yes" he said, before he realized that his thought had been silent.

~

Blood in the Snow

Late April, 1876

It was the first morning of full sunshine after a week of heavy snow. The war party had passed to the north of Bear Butte and made camp on Crow Creek, but here the water was brackish and alkaline. The creek flowed south, drawing sulfur and soda from the high plains. Tomorrow, they would cross fresh streams flowing north out of Paha Sapa, the sacred Black Hills. For now, Bear Cub would use melted snow to cook the rabbits.

There was plenty of firewood here, and some shelter from the howling night wind. Scrub pines grew on the lower slopes around them, and mature cottonwoods peppered the draws.

Breaking camp when the sun was high, they rode west. Each man had taken ash from the fire and wiped it around his eyes, but the snow was still bright.

Late the next afternoon they approached the looming pillar of Bears' Lodge, a single monolith rising more than a thousand feet into the air. The whites called it Devil's Tower. A Cheyenne elder had once told Bear Cub the story of seven girls who were playing in the woods when bears attacked. As the children fled, the ground rose beneath them and carried them far out of reach – so high that they touched the clouds and became stars. Great scars on the chimney still show where the beasts had tried to follow and had gouged the rock with their claws.

At the base of the monolith, on the east bank of the Belle Fourche, they found a red cliff to soften the wind. Here, they made camp.

The third day was warm. The men walked their horses for several hours and only mounted after crossing the Little Missouri. This was not the place to lose an animal to fatigue. Melting snow had turned the gumbo into thick, clammy gravy that stuck to their feet and accumulated as they walked. The men removed their moccasins. Their thigh and calf muscles ached, but they made progress. Steam rose from the prairie as the sun brightened, and by noon they could ride.

After two days, they reached the Powder. Here on a small hill covered with cedars, they watched campfires of the whites burning far to the south. Bear Cub counted nine fires, which meant that the train was probably big enough to have soldiers along.

Breaking camp early the next morning, they followed the river north. When their bellies ached late in the day, they stopped in the leeward side of a low bluff. Bare cottonwoods were silhouetted against the setting sun. A couple of ponies turned their heads in that direction as they picked up the familiar odor of campfires on what was now just a soft breeze.

The Sioux rode quietly to the base of the bluff and dismounted. Bear Cub and two other young boys held the ponies while the men climbed to the summit. Below, a small Crow village was spread through the trees along the eastern bank of a shallow stream, sheltered from the harsh spring wind. The stream flowed out of small hills and joined the Powder just below the village. Two dogs rummaged for food, and small children played near the water's edge. Women stood in the shelter of the trees and the Sioux warriors could hear their laughter on the breeze. An old man sat by a fire, mending arrows. There were no braves in sight, but nine ponies grazed through packed snow just north of the camp. The Powder was wide and shallow here. The Crows had camped by a ford, a decision that would cost them dearly.

Two brothers, Little Eagle and Shouts-As-He-Runs, had formed the war party. Both were veterans of innumerable forays against the Crow, Shoshone and Arapahoe, and their valor was unquestioned. For years the Sioux had been at war with these tribes, slowly forcing them west as the once vast Lakota hunting grounds became the dominion of encroaching whites.

Shouts-As-He-Runs was the first to leave the crest and make his way back down to the ponies. The others soon followed, and an animated discussion began. The older braves wanted to skirt the village, surround the small pony herd and head immediately for home. Some of the younger men felt they should at least get to ride through the village, seeing as they had come this far. It was an old argument. Young men needed the opportunity to demonstrate their bravery and daring, to enhance their stature within the tribe. This was, after all, a war party. Older, wiser heads saw only a need to protect and embellish the tribe's resources, especially now that the buffalo herds were thin and pressure on other game was higher than it had ever been. They needed to add to the pony herd, and keep the brash youngsters alive.

Little Eagle proposed a compromise. The war party would split in two. One group would ride northwest and begin driving the ponies home, while the other would raid the village.

Bear Cub grabbed the reins of his pony and followed Little Eagle and several young braves up the bluff. They stopped just shy of the summit and watched as Shouts-As-He-Runs and four older men rounded up the Crow ponies and headed north. To Bear Cub, it seemed to take a very long time. The blood pounded in his ears like the beat of a war chant, and despite the coolness of the evening, his palms were wet. Excitement masked his fear. All the games of his youth were about to become reality. He was finally going to face the enemy and take his place among the warriors.

Without a sound, Little Eagle kicked his pony into a lope and turned its head toward the village. The younger men fell in line behind him. To Bear Cub's right, Two Stones reached for an Army rifle strapped across his back. He was an unmarried brave in his mid-twenties, with a sour disposition and a fiery temper – both traits rare among the Sioux. Two Stones was a veteran of several war parties and had survived skirmishes with Crows and the Army, as well as several brushes with settlers on the Holy Road. He was as courageous as he was taciturn, but somewhat unreliable. He followed his own star and paid little heed to the elders. Some of the women whispered that he had been sired by the white agent in Fort Laramie: if he had, this in no way tempered his hatred of the settlers. He did, however, admire one aspect of the invaders' culture – their optical technology. Around his neck, on a rawhide string, he wore a short brass telescope, which he had recovered from a burning wagon on the Bozeman Trail. This, his rivals said, was the main reason behind his prowess as a hunter. Two Stones only laughed at them. He knew that the glass revealed prey at great distances, but only centuries of habit could reduce those distances to the range of a bow.

On Bear Cub's left, an untried boy of fifteen stared straight ahead and grasped the reins tightly. This was Lark's first engagement, and he was terrified. A gentle soul by nature, he feared bringing harm to others more than he worried about his own hide. He and Bear Cub had grown up together, but Lark had never shared his friend's thirst for glory. Lark lived with his grandmother, a woman skilled in ancient remedies and the lore of her tribe. His parents had both succumbed to diseases brought west by whites – soldiers from Fort Dodge, river traders plying their wares out of St. Louis and settlers traveling the Holy Road to Oregon. His grandmother's medicine had failed her daughter, but after a lifetime of service she was still held in high regard by the elders.

Little Eagle spurred his pony to a gallop. The other braves spread out behind him, each vying for the lead. Though they were still well shy of the village, some of the younger men began to yell. The din of thundering hooves and ear-splitting battle cries carried ahead of them to the closest lodges. Flaps were brushed aside and people began to appear throughout the village. As expected, they were mostly women, children and old men.

Bear Cub and Lark rode on the edge of the charge, with Lark to the outside. They were moving so fast that the ponies beneath them seemed to flow across the prairie in a smooth, even rhythm. The sound of the hooves was muted, their cries whipped away by the wind. Ahead, a large teepee loomed up right on the edge of the stream. The boys began to veer away from it when the flap opened and several Crow warriors appeared. One had a rifle, an Army issue. Even as he understood the danger, Bear Cub knew there were nine enemies before him. There had been nine horses grazing in the snow north of the village.

Lark reacted quickly, dragging his pony's head to the left and entering the stream at a gallop. He swung around the teepee and regained the bank beyond it, climbing up behind the enemy braves and out of their line of sight.

Bear Cub felt the power of the bullet when it hit, but there was no pain. The club in his left hand was made of willow, with a large round rock tied into a fork at the top, bound by rawhide. Swinging the club, he rode straight at the man with the gun, who was trying to reload. At the last second Bear Cub pulled to the right, exposing his target. Just like the ears of maize he had practiced on, he brought the rock crashing down on the man's head. There was a soft, crushing sound – not the harsh crack he was used to when the club hit a tree trunk – and the warrior dropped to his knees.

One of the Crows screamed and grabbed for the pony, but Bear Cub was moving too fast. He cleared the teepee and almost collided with Lark on the other side. They both kicked their mounts to a full gallop and made a wide arc around the village. They crossed the Powder at the ford, both praying that their ponies wouldn't lose their footing at this speed on the rocky riverbed.

As he rode, Bear Cub knew that something was wrong.

They passed the spot where the Crow ponies had been grazing and followed tracks in the snow that brought them north along the edge of the stream. Within minutes, they rejoined the main party. Shouts-As-He-Runs was driving the Crow mounts at an easy lope. He looked over his shoulder as the boys approached, staring at Bear Cub for several seconds. Then his gaze switched to Two Stones and he nodded once in the boy's direction. Two Stones fell in beside Bear Cub, never saying a word. The party continued north along the Powder until the evening faded and a full moon lit their path across the snow. They crossed the Powder at a ford just north of Buffalo Creek and headed straight west, looking for the Tongue.

Two Stones watched the ground below their hooves, where every few minutes a red drop fell from Bear Cub's blanket and colored the snow.

They made camp that night some miles shy of the Tongue and once again watched white travelers' fires in the distance. Lark looked at Bear Cub's wound. The bullet had gone clean through his shoulder, missing the bone. Cold night air and lost blood were taking their toll. Bear Cub was feeling light-headed. Lark wrapped him in several blankets and brought hot soup. He cleaned the wound and wrapped it tightly, to staunch the bleeding. Through the night, he kept a small fire burning close to Bear Cub, and pulled the blankets back over him whenever the young brave kicked them aside in his dreams.

The next morning, Bear Cub had a slight fever and his wound was bleeding again. His head had cleared but he was obviously exhausted and in no condition to ride hard. Shouts-As-He-Runs was eager to get started early, fearing the return of the Crow warriors from their hunt. He wanted to build a travois and haul Bear Cub along, but Lark insisted that it would be best to let the boy be. When Shouts-As-He-Runs ignored him, Lark volunteered to stay behind and look after the injured brave. Even this seemed unreasonable to Shouts-As-He-Runs, until Two Stones spoke up. He, too, would stay behind. He would watch for pursuit, keep the boys hidden during the days, and only let them travel under the waning moon. Lark had always thought of the fierce warrior as almost an enemy. This gift took him by surprise, but he was quick-witted enough to support the notion and Shouts-As-He-Runs was finally persuaded.

By the following evening, Bear Cub was well enough to travel some. His fever was gone and the wound had finally clotted. He was still very tired, so they decided to ride until the moon set and then make camp.

There had been no signs of pursuit. Perhaps the melting snow and the crossing of the Powder had made them harder to track, or maybe the main body of Crow men hadn't returned to their village yet and discovered the theft. On the second night, they came across heavy tracks – hundreds of shod horses riding in formation. Now they had to watch for the Army, too. There had been rumors that Yellow Hair and his cavalry were on the warpath, and that his troops had split up and were roaming the prairie in search of the people. Two Stones didn't believe it. Yellow Hair would never divide his force in Sioux country. After a decade on the plains, he knew better. It was also said that the young general often left his command and, accompanied only by his dogs, rode vast distances across the land looking for game. While Two Stones knew that the Oglala Sioux war leader Crazy Horse had similar habits, he couldn't believe that a white man could love this land enough to take such risks. Despite the vastness of the prairies, it was almost impossible to go unnoticed very long out here. Fires could be seen for miles and trails across the delicate grasslands took months, even years to heal. The only safety out here was the vastness itself. He doubted that the Crows, even if they had a good trail to follow, would bother riding for days upon end just to recover a few ponies. If they had recognized the perpetrators, they might organize a war party later, perhaps when the trees wore yellow and winter began to bite again. Not now, though.   Not so soon.

On the sixth night after Shouts-As-He-Runs had left them near the Tongue, they crested a rise and looked down on the fires of their own people.

June 25, 1876

It was good to be home.

On a broad, lazy, prairie hill, Bear Cub watched as endless miles of grass flowed in the wind. To the south and west, snow covered peaks in the Bighorns caught the morning sun. And below, sparkling as it wandered through the cottonwoods, the Little Bighorn ran between rocks like a child at play.

Bear Cub had never seen so many people gathered in one place before. There were Northern and Southern Cheyenne, Brule, Oglala, Hunkpapa – so many Sioux he didn't even recognize the tribes any more. Some three thousand of the people had come together here, spread for miles along the river in a gathering that was reminiscent of earlier ones each spring and fall in the shadow of Bear Butte. But the Paha Sapa gatherings were just family affairs. This was a meeting of the nations.

Ten years ago, Red Cloud of the Oglala Sioux had taken to the warpath in an effort to stop whites traveling the Bozeman Trail. For three summers he fought the soldiers from Fort Phil Kearney and after this war, the Hunkpapa leader Sitting Bull led the people in their defense of the Powder River country. Now, scouts had discovered that there were three columns of cavalry in the field and a council had been called to decide what to do. Some wanted to sue for peace, while most of the leaders gathered here were determined to drive the whites from the Powder.

Smoke rose from a thousand campfires, dawdling upward into the early morning sky. High atop his hill, Bear Cub wondered how far away it could be seen. His shoulder had recovered nicely and he had been rewarded for his courage and strength in fighting the Crows and the injury. With respect came responsibility. He was a lookout, a sentry. The safety of his people was in his hands. He had already gathered enough brush for a warning fire and kindling to light it.

Sioux and Cheyenne riders were chasing in and out of the camp, bearing news of the approach of Yellow Hair and his columns. The cavalry was being led here by Crow scouts and because of that, the council knew exactly where the general was and what he would do. They knew how the Crows fought. Bear Cub's task was to watch for other enemies, in blue suits or blankets, who might have skirted the camp with the intention of approaching from an unexpected direction.

As the sun moved directly overhead and the heat of the day wore on him, Bear Cub stared south. A large party of horsemen was raising dust. He struggled to see through the heat haze and the rippling air, not knowing if the riders were friends or foe. On the hill to his east, Lark sat up abruptly, his eyes glued to the south. And then, riding down the valley between the hills, Bear Cub saw to his relief that Two Stones and a small party of warriors were rushing toward his position. On the rawhide string around his neck, Two Stones wore his looking glass.

The riders were cavalry, a Major Reno's command. Custer had split his force into four groups – his own troops, an artillery train to the rear, Reno to the south, and Captain Fred Benteen to Reno's west, to create a left flank. Both Reno and Benteen commanded three troops of cavalry apiece. Custer himself, with five troops, had swung around to the north behind Bear Cub, out of sight of the bluffs. Crazy Horse knew exactly where Custer and Benteen were. Reno was a surprise. However, the veteran major did a very strange thing now, right before Bear Cub's eyes. With a long, level open field in front of him and orders to charge the camp, Reno ordered his troops to dismount and fire on the people from a great distance – almost out of range. Two Stones watched in disbelief through his looking glass, then smiled at Bear Cub, jumped on his pony and headed back down into the camp at a full gallop. The others followed and once again, Bear Cub was alone.

Some minutes later, he turned at a small sound and discovered Lark behind him. The two friends lay in the grass, watching the cavalry troops in the distance being driven back along the river. To their right, they could see Crazy Horse approach the defenders, speak with several of them, and then turn his horse's head north and kick it into a gallop. Their eyes followed him until he disappeared from sight behind a bluff. Within seconds, the sounds of a great battle could be heard. The two boys were too far away to see what was happening, but the cavalry never entered the camp so they assumed that the people were holding their own against the blue coats.

Sometime later, as the sun began to drop into the prairie north of the Bighorns, the noise of battle subsided. Below them, the camp was filling up with warriors, each one looking for his family. Unknown to the boys, the battle had devolved into a series of skirmishes washing over the plains for miles around. Custer had retreated up a bluff to their north, where he and about two hundred of his men were fighting overwhelming odds. The soldiers had been scattered.

Bear Cub and Lark ran down the hill, following the path Two Stones had taken earlier in the afternoon. From what they had seen, they understood now that their people had won the day. Laughing in sheer joy as they dodged around the sage in the draw, the boys knew that, for a while at least, the whites would retreat.

A large boulder blocked the end of the draw and they split up to skirt it, Lark taking the easier path on the left while Bear Cub climbed to the right.

The soldier behind the rock was wounded. The right leg of his uniform trousers was covered in blood. Another patch covered his stomach, and it was this that had driven him to hide in the draw. He had lost his rifle and stood now in the shadow, armed only with a short knife. He heard someone coming and, in panic and pain, he slashed viscously at Bear Cub as the boy dropped to the ground beside him. The blade grazed the boy's chest and he jumped back just before a second wild lunge connected. Now Lark descended quietly from the other side of the boulder. Before him, Bear Cub was flattened against the wall of the draw and the soldier's back was exposed. Bear Cub's eyes never left the soldier's: he didn't want to alert the enemy to Lark's presence.

The soldier, realizing that he faced a boy and not a full-grown Sioux warrior, sensed that he had the initiative here. He slowly advanced on Bear Cub, jabbing and slicing with the knife, until he was so close that the next assault could hardly fail. Bear Cub, keeping the soldier's gaze, couldn't really see what Lark was doing. He knew his friend was unarmed. Would he have enough presence of mind to pick up a rock?

Lark stood frozen. He had no personal fear for his own safety, but he could not bring himself to attack the man. Every sinew of his being screamed at him to help his friend, but something held him back. He could not strike. His legs shook with emotion and he reached for the boulder to steady himself.

Now the soldier knew. Sensing his presence, he turned quickly and drove the knife as far and as fast as he could, plunging it into Lark's belly. He lunged toward the boy, grabbed the knife with both hands and forced it up, up until it locked in the rib cage. He twisted it quickly and withdrew the blade, kicking his enemy violently with his good leg, and then turned back to face the second foe.

Bear Cub hadn't moved. He stared in disbelief, a mirror of Lark's incredulity, as his friend looked down at the wound, closed his hands over it, and sank to his knees. The soldier saw his chance. He took one final step toward Bear Cub, raised the knife high and an arrow struck him in the right cheek. Two more followed, and then Two Stones was there, falling upon the soldier before Bear Cub's instincts took over. As the warrior and soldier went to the ground, Bear Cub rushed to his friend. Still on his knees, Lark's eyes had lost their light. His dull, glazed glare never saw the ground approach as he fell forward.

Bear Cub tried to catch him.

~

A Memory of Auneau

Stretching across the front hall, wide cypress floorboards showed their age. In the hundred years since leaving Florida, they had moved endlessly with the seasons. In summer they were tight together, but in the dead of winter there were quarter-inch gaps by the door, where a cold draft snaked through. Every now and then a piece of mail dropped through the letter slot in the door, caught the draft just right, and sailed cleanly through a gap in the floor.

Mr. Harris never noticed.

He had been known as Mr. Harris ever since he came home with the Major in 1946. If he had a first name, nobody knew it.

On a warm August morning, near the village of Auneau just east of Chartres, Mr. Harris had saved the Major's life. They were fighting a German rearguard as the Allies approached Paris. Dreux, Chartres and Orleans had already been secured. On this bright Saturday morning, with the enemy in disarray and artillery quiet, a group of riflemen were enjoying fresh eggs for breakfast just yards from the Major's tent. Somebody had unearthed a henhouse during the night. Sentries were posted, but the tension of the last few weeks was quickly dissipating in the warm sunshine. In less than a week, Général de Gaulle would walk through the streets of Paris from the Arc de Triomphe all the way to Notre Dame, in front of cheering crowds.

Liberation, a whisper just a month ago, had now become a chorus.

Mr. Harris stood downwind from the group, immersed in the aroma of frying eggs. His eyes were riveted on a tree line to the north. Oak, beech and shimmering poplar reached through a pillow of bushes, while sunlight played upon their leaves. How he missed his trees! And then his eyes saw another flash, the play of light on steel. He raised his binoculars and trained them on the crotch of an enormous oak. At first he saw nothing, and then he noticed that which didn't move. Behind leaves dancing, there was a patch of darker green that was not part of the tree. When the sniper changed position, the sun at its low angle caught the nozzle of his rifle.

Mr. Harris lowered the glasses and looked around for an officer. The closest one was the Major. He would have preferred an NCO.

As he walked toward the Major, a hole appeared in the tent just to the right of the officer's head. A second later, Mr. Harris heard the shot. He broke into a run, leaping at the Major and knocking him to the ground. The second bullet entered his back.

Almost two years after Auneau, Mr. Harris drove the Major's car through the wrought iron gates of Seven Oaks. A crushed limestone driveway skirted a brick and tile gatehouse, and then meandered through the trees for a quarter of a mile to the main house.

Mr. Harris took up residence in the gatehouse and lived there for forty-one years. He drove the Major everywhere, accompanied him on excursions abroad, even bore his guns on hunting trips. He was both companion and manservant, but his real joy was in managing the woods within the walls of the estate: nineteen glorious acres with over two hundred species of trees. For generations, the Major's forebears had returned from every corner of the globe with specimens of exotic arboria: moso bamboo and Caribbean pine, monkey-pod, camphor and satinwood, even a pink ivory tree from Rhodesia. Many had succumbed to the harsh winters and some had been remanded to the sanctity of a large Victorian arboretum behind the main house. But for every one that perished, dozens had survived in the gardens and woods that separated the inhabitants of Seven Oaks from the decades passing outside their glass-topped, granite walls. And while those with a tropical lineage often grew stunted and meager, others defied all reason and raised their heads majestically above the canopy of native oaks, maples, birch and cherry. Mr. Harris was a happy man.

Once, as they drove home from a convention in Indiana - and this would be 1963, not long after the assassination - the Major asked him if he thought he'd ever marry.

"The reason I ask," he said, "is that I'd like to deed the gatehouse to you. It actually sits on its own acre of ground, you know? My grandfather built it for a tutor whom he employed, but before the title passed, the tutor was dismissed. I never learned why, exactly. There have always been rumors..."

The subject came up again during the 1972 election. Bobby Shriver was a personal friend of the Major and to everyone's surprise he ended up as McGovern's running mate. The Major had never in his life even considered voting Democrat. On a long drive to Cleveland for a fundraiser, he invited Mr. Harris into the decision.

Mr. Harris had no interest in politics, as long as they didn't concern his trees. The Major would not, could not accept that a man who had served his country, a man with a heroic streak and a love of nature, had no political philosophy. He became quite agitated when Mr. Harris revealed that in all of those times he had driven the Major to the polls, he had never actually voted.

"I'm not so sure," he said, "that a man who doesn't vote actually has the right, the moral right, to own property." And some minutes later...

"I don't think such a man should be allowed to enter City Hall and file a deed." And half-an-hour down the road...

"Let's get you registered to vote, Harris, and we'll see about the deed to the gatehouse, shall we?"

But he didn't.

Mr. Harris duly and dutifully went to the courthouse and registered as a Republican the very next morning, but that was the last he ever heard about the deed.

And now the Major was dead. After forty-one years, Mr. Harris was being told to leave his home.

He had been drawing a small pension from the estate for the past couple of years, since his sixty-fifth birthday. It was enough to live on and even enjoy a few small luxuries when combined with his Social Security check. And he had some savings in his rainy day fund, which would pay his way should he ever be hospitalized. Beyond that, he had his books, a few pieces of furniture, and his beloved trees.

Now he was being separated from those.

The new owners were a couple in their late forties. He sold used cars from a corner lot in Ashton that was lit up at night so brightly it could be seen from the main house. She wore tight black pants with red sweaters and screamed at her teenage children. Decades of seclusion were demolished in a moment the day they took possession.

It took them a week or so to notice the gatehouse, which their designer immediately decided would make a wonderful guest apartment. Their accountant was surprised to discover that the current tenant paid no rent.

An eviction notice was sent.

Mr. Harris had thirty days, it said, to vacate the only home he had known since the war. And while he was looking for alternate accommodations, the note continued, the new owners needed to access the property to carry out needed repairs.

They arrived on a Monday. Several trucks pulled up outside the gatehouse with the names of various Ashton trades people painted on their sides. Mr. Harris retired to his bedroom while they removed walls, fireplaces, light fixtures and even his cast iron claw foot bathtub - all most of a century old, and gone in minutes.

The new owners showed up to supervise. She toured the upstairs rooms with a painting contractor and he headed for the cellar with an electrician.

Alone, so completely alone in his bedroom, Mr. Harris heard every word she said. It had taken him three winters to restore the quarter-sawn white oak fireplace in the east bedroom. Two carved Italian marble sprites danced beside the flames while ebony and rosewood inlays ran around the mantle. He had paid an ironworker to repair the basket and a tile setter to rebuild the hearth with specially fired tiles to match the original ones.

She called it gaudy. A pair of trollops, she said. It wouldn't be needed with the new forced air heating, and the chimney could be used to house some of the metal ductwork. They could patch around the rest of the opening and cover it with plaster.

The tin ceiling would have to go, too.

Mr. Harris covered his face with his hands as he rocked silently back and forth on the edge of his bed.

The flooring contractor was a young man, barely thirty, who had been named Bartley because his father was late to the christening. His instructions were to remove the aged cypress floorboards and replace them with tongue and groove plywood, and linoleum. This was, after all, 1987.

There was some decay near the front door, close by the sill where a winter draft had carried in small amounts of rain, snow and sleet. This was a good place to start, he thought. The boards might be soft and the nails rusted through.

Bart began to explore with the end of a large screwdriver, and soon had a hole large enough for a claw-foot crowbar. He tapped the tool in place, stood to gain leverage and removed the first board. The second one was a bit more stubborn. Held in place with hand-forged cut nails, it had never been exposed to moisture and was as sound as the day it was installed. When he reached down to get a better grip on the crowbar, he noticed something white below the boards. Dropping to his knees, he found several pieces of mail, some old and yellowed with age and others clean, white and obviously recent. They had all, at various times, ridden that draft and slid between the wide-spaced floorboards.

Bart gathered them up and went in search of Mr. Harris. He found him in a back bedroom, his eyes red and his hair mussed when he answered Bart's knock. He took the letters in a daze, thanked the contractor and closed the door. Having met Mr. Harris a few times before, Bart wondered what had happened to the old gentleman. He was always dapper and well groomed, wearing a shirt and tie even on the warmest days of summer. Now he looked dejected, tired, and so very old.

So it was a surprise for Bart when, just a few minutes later, Mr. Harris literally ran through the house, jumped neatly over the hole in the floor and made a beeline for his car in the driveway. He wasn't sure, but Bart could have sworn that the old man was laughing.

Mr. Thomas Harcourt, a senior partner at the firm Powell, Harcourt & Lowell, had been handling the Major's affairs since his father retired from the practice in 1971. Over the years he had taken care of a couple of small, routine items for Mr. Harris as well.

When Emily knocked on Tom's office door and informed him that Mr. Harris was in the lobby and insisted on seeing him immediately, the attorney just nodded. He had no appointments until late afternoon, and he knew that old Harris wouldn't waste his time.

He recognized the envelope immediately: it was one of his own. Inside was the deed that he had executed during the Nixon administration, giving old Harris title to the gatehouse.

What, he wondered, was the problem?

~

Lobsters

A cold front swept in from the Atlantic, carrying rain across the bay. Larry O'Leary raised the collar of his coat and showed his back to the weather. He leaned into the oars and headed for shore. His currach was tar and cloth, stretched on a skeleton of steam-bent sticks. People had been building them for centuries here in west Clare. Lacking ballast, the little boat bobbed high on the waves.

Gaining the shelter of a concrete pier, Larry tied up to a mooring buoy. Then, with his two lobster pots in one hand, he reached for a rusty ladder in the side of the pier and clambered up. On top, the wind was becoming fierce. Larry leaned into it as he walked to the shelter of the boathouse, holding his cap in place with his spare hand.

Inside the boathouse, an elderly man sat close by a barrel stove, his arms extended to embrace its heat. The aroma of a briar pipe clenched between his teeth brought water to Larry's mouth. Pulling the lobsters out of the pots, he dropped them in a deep basin of salt water in the sink by the window. Then, nodding acknowledgment of the old man's greeting, he reached into a pocket for his own pipe.

"Tis a lazy wind," the old man said, "that would sooner go through you than around you."

Larry agreed, adding that the wind had caused him to come in before recovering all of his pots. The two he had managed to pull held just three lobsters, and he already had customers for at least five. Well, it couldn't be helped. One of those Yanks up at the Stella Maris Lodge would just have to settle for steak tonight, God bless him.

Larry and the old man smoked contentedly in silence for a few minutes. Outside, the sky became darker and the wind howled around them. As the old man stoked the fire, a delicious smell of burning peat reminded Larry that he hadn't eaten yet today. He got up and searched the boathouse but, despite the fact that there were plenty of cooking utensils, there was no evidence of food. Thinking that he could perhaps make it home before the rain, he walked to a window to assess the weather. But by now he was too late. The wind was dying and large drops spattered on the concrete pier. As he watched, the drops turned to sheets of icy water.

This was not how August was supposed to be in the west of Ireland. By now the lodges and hotels along the Strand were full of tourists who came here seeking sunshine and the famous white sands of Boland's beach. The town was so full that Larry himself had even managed to find a family to share his cottage. A dentist from Dublin had paid for two week's stay. Father Brian had arranged it all and, though the dentist had paid his money up front, the wise old priest had only given half to Larry. The other half was due when the dentist left, provided he was happy enough with the way he had been treated.

Now the dentist and his family were shut up in two little rooms against the weather, and Liam could imagine the scene. The children, bored, are sitting by the window, watching rivulets of water race down the glass. The window fogs and they begin to make pictures. The boy draws a train and has run out of space. He brings the tracks to the edge of his pane, and then jumps the muntin and continues on his sister's side. Now a pushing match begins and this quickly escalates into a free-for-all. The dentist, deprived of a day on the links, is not in the mood to tolerate a racket. He shouts at the girl to stop hitting her brother. But his wife has been paying more attention and she knows about the railway's illicit new branch line.

A word from the old man brought Larry back to the boathouse. He was holding out a flask, offering a drink. In the absence of food, Larry welcomed it. The fiery whiskey warmed his belly, but did little for his hunger.

The old man was a distant relative of Larry's, some sort of cousin on his Uncle Noel's side. Noel was long dead, but his son, Philly, was still living and had a grand house in Dublin. As far as Liam knew, these and some distant American cousins were all that was left of the O'Learys.

When Noel died he had left nothing to Philly but a huge cast iron stove. Shortly thereafter, Philly was offered a government job in Dublin, and in 1963 he left County Clare for good. The stove found its way to Larry's cottage because it was too heavy for the trip to Dublin. It now occupied one whole wall of Larry's kitchen and, when fired up in the winter, its great mass heated the cottage from dusk to dawn without his having to feed turf to it in the middle of the night.

Larry, though a rag and bone man by trade, made a few Euros on the side every summer running his lobster pots. He had come by the currach in the course of conducting his business, and had decided that it had potential. Fergus O'Toole, a giant of a man who farmed three fields down by the shore just north of Kilbeggan, had lost his son to a storm. The boy had been out in this very same currach collecting kelp for the fields, and an east wind had crept up on him. He was out beyond the islands in an open sea and by the time he realized that the storm was coming, it was too late. The currach had washed up in Boland's Bay two days later, but the boy's body was never found.

At times Larry felt uneasy in the currach, remembering the fate of Michael O'Toole. He was often reluctant to leave the relative safety of the bay, and on a day such as this he was quick to seek shore at the first signs of a storm. But there were other times, days full of sunshine when he sat upon the bobbing sea and felt completely at peace in the boat. Sometimes he even sensed the presence of the boy, and welcomed his company.

The old man snorted, then rolled a dollop of phlegm to the middle of his tongue. He spat with practiced ease and his projectile sailed neatly through the opening in a brass spittoon next to the stove. Larry was impressed.

"Have you ever gone for lobsters?" he asked.

"Indeed I have not," the old man replied. "The good Lord gave me feet, not fins. I have no business out there on the water."

"If you don't like the sea," said Larry, "what are you doing down here in the boathouse?"

"Tis not the sea I dislike," he said with a smile. "Tis the water. I was down at O'Meara's picking up my newspaper and an ounce of tobacco, and I saw the storm coming. It looked slower than it was, and I thought I could beat it home. It caught up with me outside."

Liam nodded, and the two of them sat smoking in silence for a few minutes. Then Larry had a thought.

"Have you ever been beyond in Dublin?" he asked. "You know, up at Philly's house."

"I have," the old man replied, nodding his head vigorously. "And I'll tell you something. It was a strange day indeed."

"Strange?" asked Larry. "In what way?"

"Well, maybe it would be a good thing if you knew. After all, you're the last of the family hereabouts. Someone should carry our version of the truth with him, in case people ever heard otherwise."

The old man had Larry's undivided attention. Was he about to tell of a family disgrace? Had Philly done some terrible deed? A murder, perhaps. Or, God forbid, something even worse! Had he robbed a Church maybe, or bet against Clare in the All-Ireland football final? Larry's mind raced through the ugly possibilities.

"It's funny that you should bring lobsters in here tonight," the old man said. "For it was lobsters that started the whole trouble."

"Lobsters?" Larry was at a loss. How could lobsters cause a family scandal?

"It was maybe four or five years after Philly moved to Dublin. 1968, perhaps. I was above at the forge with our blind pony that was being shod by Brian Dolan. Now, Brian had a notion to take the train up to Dublin and see the Spring Show. He loved horses, and the pick of the world's steeds would be above in Ballsbridge. He wanted company, and sure wasn't I free?"

"Did ye catch the train in Ennis?"

"We did, the following morning. I thought Philly might put us up for a couple of nights, and by way of rent, I suggested we bring along a few Atlantic lobsters for Philly and the wife, just so we didn't show up empty-handed. Well, the problem with lobsters, as you know, is that they have to be alive when you boil them. So Brian had this wonderful plan to also transport a little bit of the Atlantic Ocean on the train to Dublin. How to accomplish this in those days, before everything was plastic, stumped him for a little while. And then he hit upon an idea. Being a smith's apprentice, he decided to weld up a small waterproof tank with two handles, and he spent most of the night before the trip doing just that.

"The following morning Brian was up before the sun, buying lobsters on the pier. He got five of them into his tank, filled it to the top with salt water, and attached the lid tightly."

"Didn't they need air?"

"Now, son, who's telling this story? Anyway, by breakfast we were sitting in the station at Ennis waiting for the 9.05 to Connolly in Dublin. I was eating a scone and Brian was staring at his tank. He had the same thought you just did.

'Do you think they can breathe?' he asked me.

"Fish don't like too much air," I replied.

'No,' he said. 'I mean, do you think there's enough oxygen in the water to keep them alive all the way there?'

"And just as he said this, the Express pulled into the station and we hauled our unlikely luggage aboard. By the time we were seated, his mind had wandered to other things. But just outside Limerick Junction he looked again at the tank.

'I'm going to check on them,' he said.

"Do you think that's wise?" said I.

'I do,' he said, and with that he pried the lid loose. No sooner had he done so than the engineer hit the brakes for our stop at the Junction. The tank flew from his grasp and slid between the seats to the end of the carriage. Just as it reached the door, the conductor entered. He was about to announce the stop when a pot full of live lobsters descended on him. His eyes opened wide and he let out a bloodcurdling yell! The lobsters, smelling freedom, made a run for it."

"Sure, lobsters aren't that frightening," Larry said.

"They are when they appear on a train," the old man laughed. "Passengers scattered before them, but they were probably more afraid of the cowardly conductor than the snapping claws. When it was all sorted out, Brian and I were deposited on the platform at Limerick, lobsterless, and banned forever from all conveyances owned or operated by the C.I.E."

"Did you ever get to Dublin?"

"We did, of course," he said. "We hitch-hiked up the road and we were there before the train".

Larry laughed. The rain was still coming down in torrents and he realized that he was hungrier now than ever.

"Damn the Yanks," he muttered. He found a cast iron pot under some old fishing nets by the sink, and filled it with water. When it boiled, he dropped in two of the lobsters. Within minutes, he and the old man were feasting on the Americans' supper. It tasted so good that they boiled up the third one, too.

The storm died down as they finished eating. Larry stepped from the boathouse into a beautifully clear, chilly evening. The old man followed him outside and stood looking to the east, where the last of the clouds were approaching the horizon.

"D'ya fancy a drink?" the old man asked.

"I do indeed," said Larry, and he turned towards town and the warmth of the pub.

"You'll have to buy," said the old man, a twinkle in his eye. "Sure I don't have a penny on me."

Larry smiled to himself. The old man was indeed his kin.

The Apple Man

Dublin, 1973

The first time he took a 48A bus all by himself, Michael was eleven years old. He watched it approach the bus stop, roaring through potholes and ponds on the Ballinteer Road, a green-painted, double-decked monster covered in ads. It would be a full year until he got long pants and Dublin this November was awfully cold, so he was glad to leap aboard.

An open platform at the back of the bus offered the choice of a doorway to the lower level, or a scary climb up a winding metal staircase. No self-respecting boy would sit with the housewives and old-age pensioners downstairs, so Michael grabbed the shiny handrail and began to climb up top. He almost lost his grip as the bus lurched around the bend outside the Old Mens' Home, its roof scraping the overhanging chestnut boughs as it shuddered through the turn, never slowing a whit. Down the hill it roared: there were no more bus stops here, and the driver floored the pedal until the old diesel screamed.

The passengers were silent. They knew the routine. Michael sat hard on the first seat available and grabbed the edge of it with both hands. The conductor noticed him right away and clicked out a sixpenny return ticket. Michael reluctantly paid him.

A hundred yards past Dundrum Castle, in the middle of a gray granite bridge and a sudden downpour, the driver began to brake. Michael could see the Church of the Holy Cross to his left, and the sprawling wound of the Pye factory to his right – a tin building in an ancient stone village. The bus slid into the intersection on Sandyford Road, barely slowing as it made a sharp left around Campbell's Shoe Shop, and pulled to a stop at the shelter in front of the church.

Michael used both handrails to slide down the stairs. As he jumped off the platform, the 48A was already moving toward the city center, six miles away. The ad on the back of it was for Players cigarettes, which reminded Michael that he had neither a smoke nor a chance of one. He only had sixpence left of his own money, and that was for the return ticket on the next bus, the 86.

The walk up the hill on the other side of the village was steep. He was already out of steam when he passed the Garda Station a little way up, with the National School across the road. This wasn't a good place to get tired: some of those National School boys were pretty tough, and they might be getting out for lunch any minute now. They'd take his money as soon as look at him.

He turned his eyes back to the path and forced himself up the hill. He had the day off himself because his teacher, Mrs. Brophy, was having a baby and the new teacher couldn't start work until next Monday.

Just shy of the top, he again looked across the road. There was your man's apple tree, the one in the sunken garden where he'd been caught two weeks ago robbing the orchard. Up the tree he was with a duffle bag full of apples when his sister and all her friends let out a series of shrieks and took off running. Michael abandoned the bag, dropped to the ground and ran for his life – which wasn't worth much when his mother found out that he's lost his duffle. He went back, tear-streaked and timid, and knocked on the door. Your man answered it, rubbed his head, and then handed Michael the bag.

It was full of apples!

They shared a conspirators' smile. Snatching victory from the jaws of defeat, he thought (a phrase from his Boy's Book of Adventure, the one that Granny had given him in June for his birthday). He vowed he'd never rob this decent gentleman again.

This year, anyway.

It was a pity about the bike, though. This hill had given him one great gift and taken another, all in the space of a couple of weeks. He could almost see Peter Calally now, racing ahead of him down the hill, head down and feet spinning faster than a windmill in a gale. The rain sprayed around his legs where the bicycle clips kept his pants out of the chain. Michael clicked his bike into third gear, bent his head and followed Peter down the hill to perdition or glory: it didn't really matter which. When he looked up again, there was a light blue

Volkswagon a few feet ahead, stopped at the traffic light. He pulled the brakes with all his might, but the rain robbed him of traction. So he leaned back in the saddle to distance himself from the collision.

The front wheel of the bike was ruined and the forks were bent. There wasn't a scratch on the Volkswagon.

The driver, an elderly woman from Rathmines, was so relieved to see him cry that she bundled him into the car and took him home. Which, of course, screwed up any chance he had to tell a good lie about the shape the bike was in.
Michael's father went back for the bike and got so upset at the sight of it that he had to stop in at Dundrum House for a pint, just to calm himself.

Cresting the top of the hill, he spied the stop for the 86 Bus, the one that ran all the way to Stillorgan. They'd told him in school that the name came from a saint called Lorcan who had built a church there. John Mooney said it came from the saint's whatcha, because now that he was dead he had a still organ. Poor Mooney had to go to the Boss for that one – up those plastic tiled steps to the office on the second floor, where Brother Brendan stood with his back to the door, watching traffic on the Kilmacud Road. Six belts with the leather strap, and Mooney never cried. He said later he was still laughing inside and that's what made him strong.

The second bus was a smoother ride. The road was straight and in good repair. His father had said that it was because the mayor's brother lived here, but Michael didn't know which house. There weren't too many – this was still almost the countryside until the bus turned north again and came to a stop near the shopping center in Stillorgan. Two blocks past the center, he spied Finlay's Bicycle Shop on the right hand side. He felt in his pocket for his father's money; three pounds to pay for the new forks and rim. Well, not exactly new. The bicycle shop had a big pile of bits and pieces out back and if you sorted through them and found the parts you wanted, old man Finlay would sell them cheap. Brand new forks would have cost a week's worth of porter.

Finlay was ancient, at least fifty, and he wore a cap that was shiny from the wearing. He had on a threadbare tweed jacket that smelled a little like horses, and the aroma grew somewhat more pungent as he wrestled with the half-a-bike that Michael had dragged in from outside. His shop was heated with a large coal stove and in front of that lay a dog that was old enough to have played with Jesus. Michael absently scratched his ears while Finlay freed the forks. The dog looked up at him with the same soft expression he had seen in the eyes of the apple man.

On the way home, he wrestled the new forks and rim from one bus to the other, parking his parts in adjacent seats when there was room. It was late in the day and the buses were crowded with people coming home from their jobs in town. Alighting at his final stop, he almost fell off the platform as both arms were busy carrying treasures and he had no hold on the bus. A big hand reached out and steadied him. It was the apple man.

"Did the getaway car fall apart then?" he asked, smiling and nodding at the bicycle parts. The conductor, climbing nimbly down the spiral stairs behind Michael, laughed and said that it would be a slow vehicle indeed if a man wanted to outrun the Guards.

"Oh, I'm not so sure," the apple man said. "You don't recognize this desperado, do you? He's a wanted man. A ferocious gangster, he is. Why, I once saw him with my very own eyes make a clean getaway with a big bag full of loot."

Michael jumped off the platform and the apple man waved goodbye, a huge grin on his face.

It took his father most of the evening to fix the bike, but the following day was Saturday and as soon as he had downed his porridge, Michael headed for the shed and a test drive. All day long and most of the next, he rode furiously around the neighborhood. It seemed to him that the front wheel was smoother and faster and rounder than any he had ever seen, and the new forks led the bike through curves and circles with a grace and precision he had never known before. His father laughed and said it was just an old bike, but he stood by the gate and watched until Michael disappeared around the bend at the end of the street.

On Sunday night, he washed the bike. Every inch of it. He scrubbed and sponged until it gleamed and then he coated the entire frame with a thin veneer of oil. The black frame glistened in the glare of the shed's only bulb. A hero's bike. He almost burst with the joy of it, and then another thought struck him. How could God give such a bike to the kind of a boy who would steal apples from a decent man? The kind of man who would catch a fellow falling from a bus. Was it a test, he wondered? Was Jesus up there looking over the edge of his cloud, watching how Michael was behaving? Had He made a mark in his book when Michael failed to mention stealing apples in Confession? And now there was pride, a Deadly Sin. In the space of a fortnight, he had gone from misdemeanors to felonies.

The more he thought of it, the gloomier he got. By the time he went to bed, he couldn't look at the bike any more. Every glimpse of it made him ashamed. So much so that, when morning sunshine swam across the rooftops, he decided to walk to school. It was a good day for a walk with hardly a cloud in the sky.

He arrived as the first bell rang across the schoolyard. Footballs and airplanes disappeared into rucksacks as a hundred and eighty-two children streamed through the doors with various levels of enthusiasm. He sat in his usual desk, three back from the front and as far from Jimmy Scanlon as he could possibly get without leaving the room. The malaise was still upon him and even the excited conversation of a Monday morning couldn't rock him free of it. He reluctantly reached for the geography book in his bag on the floor and, as he straightened up, he saw a very strange sight. There was a sack on the teacher's table – a big one, the likes of which you'd see outside Garrett's Grocery, filled with onions or carrots or spuds and such. Only this one was open at the top, and spilling across the desk were several large, red, ripe apples. And Michael knew without looking, when the door opened and the new teacher entered, exactly who it would be.

Outside, the last few clouds dissipated in the east and the glory of warm November sunshine filled the classroom.

A good day, he thought, for a bike ride.

~

The Suit

The stone floor of the cottage was icy cold as Paddy stood by the toilet. He relieved himself while staring into a tired old mirror that could no longer return his gaze. Seeing no stubble, he decided not to shave.

A pot of Flahavan's porridge sat on a burner of the black stove. Stoking the embers, he threw in a handful of peat and a couple of twigs, and then worked the carpet bellows until life grew inside. He poured a little buttermilk over the porridge, added a fist of brown sugar and worked the compound until it began to give. Holding the pot under the pump, Paddy dribbled in a little water and replaced his breakfast upon the burner to heat. While it did, he sat on the end of his low trundle bed, rubbing warmth into his feet before pulling on his holy black socks.

The porridge began to pop and boil as Paddy reached under the bed for his heavy leather brogues. After breakfast, he left the empty pot with several others in the chipped enamel sink and walked out to the shed where a pony stood silent in a darkened stall. Using the side of his brogue to scoot some soiled straw aside, he revealed a patch of bare dirt and threw down some hay. As the pony ate, Paddy took the harness from a peg on the wall and unraveled it. In a little while he harnessed the pony, backed him out of the shed and led him between the shafts of a flatbed cart. The pony stood obediently as Paddy opened the yard gate and climbed up on the cart. A brief shake of the reins and they were on their rounds.

Paddy O'Leary had been a rag and bone man since he was nine years old, following in his father's steps and those of his grandfather before him.

This was Tuesday, so Paddy drove the pony out along the north road to Kilbeggan. They climbed gentle hills until he could look down upon the entire valley, where stone walls divided green pasture from meadow. A small white cottage graced every third or fourth field, with smoke rising from each hearth as the woman of the house baked the day's bread. Alongside the winding road was a small ditch dug by the Council, maybe a foot deep and hardly that wide. Yesterday's rain flowed down the hill inside the little ditch, pushing up wildflowers as it ran. This was a peaceful enough journey for Paddy, only occasionally interrupted by a barking dog or a housewife bringing her cast-offs to the cart and choosing among its bounty for her payment.

There was only one house left before the cart would begin its descent into the shelter of Kilbeggan valley. As he passed it, the widow Nelson hailed Paddy from her upstairs window. He stopped and waited and soon she came out and loaded a bunch of old gramophone records into the cart. In return, she chose a big ball of brown string that he had found behind the creamery, the kind you'd use to tie up rubbish for a rag and bone man.

Halfway down the hill into Kilbeggan, Paddy drove the pony off the main road and through a pair of impressive granite gateposts sporting a dense beard of ivy. The pony made its way along an overgrown, winding driveway and soon Paddy could see the Lodge ahead. Once the social center of the parish, if not the county, the stately home was beginning to look dowdy and tired. The same, thought Paddy, could be said of its owner.

He dropped the reins in front of the house, threw a sop of hay to the pony and made his way to the side door. Mrs. McBride herself answered his knock and invited him into the kitchen. She was alone today, she said, it being Cook's day off. She asked if he'd like a cup of tea, so he sat himself down in a wooden rocking chair beside the stove. Despite the sunny day, the house still held the morning's damp and he welcomed the warmth.

When the tea was brewed, she placed two dainty china cups on an old tin tray. Between the cups she set a small plate of freshly buttered scones, a little jar of jam with the lid screwed off, and a silver spoon. Paddy's mouth began to water as he sat patiently waiting for his share, all the while stirring the tea and shamefully aware of his own smell in the presence of such a fine lady. He moved back a bit from the fire and that helped some.

She asked him how he was doing. Was the weather good or bad for trade? She wondered if he was going to Mass on Sundays, as she hadn't seen him there in a while. The trade was good, he said, not great, and he explained that he was in the habit of standing in the back of the church with the other bachelors so she might not have seen him from her pew up front. But he was there regularly, and that's the truth.

Then, she did a strange thing. After looking at him quizzically for a minute, Mrs. McBride stood up and asked him to do likewise. Again she looked at him, this time from head to toe, and left the room. He stood there in this strange, clean kitchen, wondering if he were allowed to sit down. No sooner had he done so than she returned. In her arms she bore a wool suit, a grey one with tiny flecks of black and brown, a quality article and she handled it accordingly. As Paddy again rose to his feet, she held the suit up to him and clucked admiringly as she pulled it this way and that to see if it would fit. Finally, she gave it to him, saying that he had no need to skulk by the back door of St. Michael's any more, that he could come and sit up front like a regular person. She advised taking a bath before donning the suit, but looked him in the eye as she said that, so he took no offense.

Thanking her, he laid the suit gently on the kitchen table. Then they sat by the stove in silence a while, enjoying a communion that transcended their different stations. Paddy didn't often feel comfortable with people: he knew that most of them only saw his soiled clothes and his loneliness.

After a few minutes, she asked him if he had ever met her husband. Yes, he said, he had once, back when the Colonel was still just Major McBride. Paddy said that he had admired the man but, like many people hereabouts, didn't know if he approved of an Irishman, even a Protestant, fighting for the Queen. She nodded at that, glad of his honesty, and agreed that she had often wondered about it herself. Then she told him about her husband. He could hear the love in her voice and once again in this kitchen he felt a little shame.

She told him of her husband's passing. He had been grouse hunting, she said, with some cousins down from Dublin for the weekend. There was an accident—his own gun. He didn't suffer, and she was glad of that. Then she turned to Paddy and, nodding at the suit, told him that McBride had been wearing that very suit an hour before he went hunting that fateful day. Paddy smiled politely, suppressing a shudder.

At noon, a clock in the back parlor proclaimed the hour with a Westminster chime. Paddy suddenly remembered that the pony had been outside all this time in the sun. He thanked her for the suit and the tea, and set out on his way to O'Brien's pub. He led the pony down Kilbeggan hill, not jumping aboard the cart until the road leveled off.

Half a mile shy of the village, Paddy reached into the back of the cart and pulled the fine wool suit into the seat beside him. Turning the jacket inside out, he felt the silk lining and read the London tailor's label. The sun was hotter now, so he took off his soiled tweed cap and set the heavy suit aside. As he did so, he noticed the corner of a folded yellow envelope sticking out of the change pocket. An excitement came over him. He reached for the envelope, sure it was money. Why else would it be in the change pocket? But as soon as he had it in his hand, he knew that it wasn't.

The envelope was addressed in a shaky hand to Caitlin McBride. Inside was a note, still white when set against the yellowed envelope. The note was just one page long, written on Lodge stationery, and read:

My Dearest Caitlin,

There are times in our lives when we must be strong. I, to my shame, am no longer able to do so. The good doctor informs me that I have but weeks. Two or three months at the outside. Each day the pain increases and his potions and powders do little to alleviate it.

I have faced death a dozen times on the battlefield, but until now I have never felt cold fear. I don't wish to die slowly, and I don't want you to watch me die.

Your cousins from Dublin will be here for the grouse in an hour or two.

I hope you can find it in your heart to forgive me.

I have always loved you.

William.

Though Paddy looked up when he was done reading, it was several moments before he noticed that the cart had stopped. He snapped the reins and the pony walked to the hitching post outside O'Brien's. There it stood silently while he fetched a nosebag of oats from the back of the cart.

Inside the pub, Paddy chose the darkest corner he could find. He sat there gazing at a fresh pint of Guinness until the creamy white head began to merge into the strong black stout below.

The next Sunday, Paddy O'Leary got out of bed at eight o'clock. He pulled a galvanized steel washtub into the kitchen, filled it up with soapy water and took a bath in front of the big black stove. Despite the fact that it was July, he dressed in his new wool suit. Then he walked down the middle of the main street to nine o'clock mass at St. Michael's, ignoring the taunts of neighbor children as he passed them in his finery. He arrived five minutes early and strode confidently down the aisle to the pew occupied by the Widow McBride. He genuflected and entered the pew, kneeling on the worn pine board. He didn't bow his head.

As the parish priest walked out on the altar, the widow leaned towards Paddy. She reached her left hand into the change pocket of the suit. For a moment, her face registered panic. Then, as they looked into each other's eyes, each slowly smiled.

~

A Terrible Beauty

"All changed, changed utterly:
A terrible beauty is born."

William Butler Yeats, Easter 1916

On Summit Hill, the bronze bells of St. Paul's cathedral rang the hour. In a gray van passing below, the driver glanced at his dashboard clock. Obeying the speed limit, the van moved down Summit Avenue past stately Victorian mansions, and then turned north into meaner streets. On reaching Superior Close, the headlights died. Rolling to a stop outside number 325, two men alighted and approached the house.

Through the open living room window, the driver could see five men in their thirties and forties gathered around a television. One spoke with a strong Dublin accent.

"Hush now, lads. Here it is."

He turned up the volume on a local newscast.

"In Northern Ireland today" a male announcer said, "a shootout between terrorists and police has cost four people their lives. The incident happened in the town of Newry, where a car carrying three off-duty policemen was ambushed by the Provisional IRA. A spokesman for Sinn Fein, the political arm of the IRA in Dublin, has issued a statement claiming the attack was in retaliation for the death of terrorist Michael Doherty, 26, who died last week in unexplained circumstances in a Belfast jail. Aside from the policemen, a British soldier who came to their aid was also gunned down."

The man turned off the set with a flourish.

"A British soldier was gunned down!" he said. "They make it sound like a criminal act."

"Mick Doherty being murdered in his cell," said another, a big man with a red beard. "Now there's a criminal act for you, Liam". There was a chorus of agreement.

Liam looked through the living room doorway to an open staircase where a boy of ten watched the men through the railings.

"Are you not in bed yet?" Liam asked. " I thought I told you to be off an hour ago. The talk of fellas like your uncle Seamus is not for your ears, son."

"Is the young one still not in bed?" the big man asked. Then, laughing, "Shall I wallop him for you, Liam?"

The father walked out to the stairway and stood below the boy. "Off to bed now, son," he said gently. "You'll learn nothing from these old Fenians that'll do you much good in America."

There was a sound at the back of the house and, as Liam turned towards it, the front door crashed open behind him.

Two men in ski masks were framed in the doorway. Two more came from the kitchen at the back of the house. The hallway filled with staccato bursts of gunfire. Within seconds, all five men in the house were down.

One of the gunmen walked into the living room where Seamus lay groaning on the floor. He reached into his back pocket and withdrew a small Luger. He knelt, aimed the pistol at the back of Seamus' head and fired. Then he walked to each of the other men and did likewise.

None of the gunmen had spoken a single word: all communication had been accomplished with hand signals. Now the man with the pistol stood up, looked around the room and signaled to the others to withdraw. They left quickly, heading out the front door toward the van.

The man with the pistol began to back out of the room, checking for pulses as he moved toward the door. In the hallway, he stood over Liam's body and prodded his limp form with the silver-capped toe of a snakeskin cowboy boot.

"You always were a loser, Liam," he said in a quiet Irish accent. Then he turned on his heel and ran to the van.

The boy, still crouched in darkness, stared wide-eyed at the carnage.

Outside, the van squealed around the corner at the end of the street. Lights were coming on in several houses as curious neighbors began reacting slowly to what had sounded like a car backfiring. A woman and her twelve-year-old daughter were a block east of the Close, walking hand-in-hand on their way home from Girl Scouts. At the sound of the tires, they stopped and looked at the van. The woman turned her eyes to the house, then back to the van, and broke into a run.

~2013~

Most of the yards in Superior Close were well kept. The city had recently installed new sidewalks beneath the towering rows of copper maples, and Summit Hill was experiencing what real estate brokers called revitalization.

Morning sunlight dancing on the white clapboards of number 325 found Liam junior asleep on a queen-size waterbed. An alarm clock rang and he reached out lazily to shut it off.

When he got downstairs to the kitchen his mother, Moira, was already cooking breakfast.

"Sleep well, son?"

"Like a lamb, Mom."

"I didn't hear you come in. I stayed up for Leno. Did you get home very late?"

"About three, I think. A few of us from the office went out to that new club in the Mall of America. There was a good band, so we stayed."

"Heaven forbid that I sound like a mother, but isn't three o'clock in the morning a bit late when you have to get up and face your boss?"

"Jerry was there too. He can't yell at me anyway. I'm his bright shining boy this month."

"Was that girl there, that Nancy?"

"Yes Mom, that Nancy was there." He stressed the word 'that', a little annoyed. His mother picked up on his tone and switched gears.

"Why are you in such favor with Jerry this month?"

"Some hackers found a way to access ATMs. I got the story before the big boys at the Trib."

"What in God's name does that mean?" She put a plate of food in front of him. "I wish you'd speak English, son."

"It's nearly eight. Gotta run, Mom." He grabbed his jacket, a worn brown briefcase and a slice of toast, kissed Moira and headed for the door.

"What time will you be home?" she asked.

"Early. Unless that Nancy leads me astray. Perhaps I can talk her into it!"

Liam found a parking spot in front of the ancient Dispatch building and, whistling to himself, ducked through the revolving doors. An elevator took him from the foyer to his office on the ninth floor. The room was open plan, and it felt cavernous and impersonal this early.

He sat in his swivel chair, hit a button on the keyboard, spun the chair to survey the office, and then turned back to the screen to settle down to work. The office filled up around him. An hour or so later his editor, Jerry Williams, walked by. He was holding a file.

"In my office."

A co-worker turned to Liam and grimaced theatrically. Liam feigned fear as he followed his boss through the maze of desks.

"Late start, Jerry?"

"Shut the door."

Jerry rummaged in his suit for Tums. He was forty-six but tried hard to act younger. The late night had taken a toll.

"We may have another ATM story for you". He tossed the file on his desk and Liam reached for it. A minute passed, then another.

"Jesus!" Liam closed the file.

"I know. The bastards got away with almost twelve million."

"How did they get in?"

"Two of them held the bank manager's wife at gunpoint in his home. It's an hour or so north of the city, in a suburb called Theydon Bois. The other two drove him to the bank, used his clearance to get in, and then forced him to use his security code to access the mainframe."

"Did they hurt his wife?"

"No."

"Well, that's something."

"Perhaps. They shot him."

"Why?"

"Who knows? Perhaps he saw something, someone's face maybe. Perhaps he heard a voice. Do they need a reason?"

"This is a little out of my line, Jerry. Are you asking me to work it?"

"Yes."

"Why?"

"Because they're Irish."

"So . . ."

"You have connections. You know people. Nobody else in this office has ever even been there, at least nobody on the team."

"Aw, come on, Jerry! I was in Ireland once, for a two-week vacation. My parents came from there, not me. Shit, I don't even remember it. I was fourteen years old!"

"But you have family in Ireland. Your mother does. You could make the connections. We need somebody who can run a computer, true. But we also need somebody who can read the political climate, ask a few favors from the locals, get in with the Irish cops."

"Gardai."

"What?"

"Gardai. That's what they call the cops. The Gardai."

"That's what I mean! You speak the language. Anyway, there's another reason I need you."

"What's that?"

"You're fresh off a similar ATM story, and you seem to understand the technical aspects."

"Yeah, but we don't even have an angle. I mean, this happened in London."

"Uhuh. But Prime Bank's headquarters is here in St. Paul. A lot of our readers bank with them."

"Okay, I'll buy that." Liam was silent for a minute. Something was missing here. Jerry didn't need to send a reporter to Europe to cover a foreign bank robbery, even one with a strong local angle. He could just pull the updates off the wire and send some raw recruit out to Prime for comments and mugshots.

"What are you leaving out, Jerry?"

"They got the access profiles for Prime Bank's ATMs."

"Wow!"

"And they've started using them."

"Where?"

"Cash machines in London, Birmingham, Dublin and Amsterdam. We're not sure, but we think they may have accessed a machine at Logan Airport yesterday."

"Well, with the access profiles, they can probably make their own cards."

"That's what our boy at Prime said, too."

"Did he tell you that the profiles give them access to PIN numbers?"

"Yeah. He says that's not a problem. The bank will stop issuing new cards until this is over. Can't be more than a week or two, right? And they're instructing their computers to decline cash requests on cards issued yesterday or later. They also programmed the ATMs to confiscate any new cards that show up, and everybody is being asked to create a new PIN. Why are you shaking your head?"

"It's not new cards they have to worry about, Jerry. With the access profiles, they can make cards for existing accounts."

Jerry stopped to let this sink in. It didn't.

"You mean they can rob Prime's customers... and there's nothing the bank can do about it?"

"Pretty much. There would be no way to tell a counterfeit card from an existing, authentic one. At least, not the first time it was used."

"How about when they come back to the well? If they use the same card twice?"

"These guys are pros, Jerry. They're not going to do that. If they did, the cops would have a good chance at them, and they know that. No, they're going to use each card once, and throw it."

"What do these access profiles look like?"

"Just a bunch of numbers. A list. They're usually generated by a mainframe and backed up on CDs or flash-drives. A whole set probably fits on a single CD. There's only one thing Prime can do now. They'll have to cancel all the cards they've ever issued and close all the accounts."

"No bank can do that, Liam. Not even Prime. Think what that would do to customer confidence. Hell, if we print a story on that, they'll have an old-fashioned run on the bank. So far, they have a few isolated customers who've been taken and they've already covered those losses. They won't want to tell the world they have a problem."

"Then the only way out for them is to find the CDs."

"Then I guess you're going to Ireland. That's where they'll be looking, so that's where the story is. I'll have your plane ticket here by noon. Go home and pack and I'll have Accounts get you some Euros. Anything else you need?"

Liam smiled. "No, Jerry. I have my Prime cash card if anything comes up!"

Delta flight 423B was only five minutes late when it touched the tarmac in Dublin. As Liam walked up the ramp from the gate, he saw an attractive woman in her early thirties wearing a bland business suit and holding a sign bearing his name.

Liam waved at the woman and pointed to himself. She gestured towards the end of the railing that divided them, and he worked his way in that direction.

"Welcome to Ireland, Mr. McMahon"

"Thank you. And you are . . ."

"Sheila Walsh. Mr. Williams in Minnesota asked me to meet you. I'm with the Dublin Post, but I string for a couple of Yank rags."

"Good old Jerry. Efficient as ever."

"Have you any bags with you?"

"This" he indicated a large piece of carry-on, "and one that I checked. Do you know where baggage claim is?"

"I do indeed. It's right along here. I'll tell you what: I'll go ahead and bring the car up while you go through customs. How's that sound?"

"Actually, we've already done customs in Shannon. But you go ahead and get your car and I'll claim my luggage. Perhaps you could tell me where to meet you?"

"Oh, sure you can't miss me. It's a small enough airport. I'll just be out front, arguing with a guard about where I should wait. Don't be too long now."

"I'll try not to be."

Sheila Walsh turned towards the front of the terminal and Liam began to make his way to the baggage claim area. As he walked, a sixtyish, longhaired but well dressed man fell in step beside him.

"Welcome home, Mr. McMahon."

"Do I know you?"

"My name is Connolly, Mr. McMahon. Richard Connolly. Dick, to my friends. I was a great friend of your Da many years ago, God rest his soul."

"You've done well to keep in contact with him."

"I beg your pardon?"

"Nobody outside my office knew I was coming to Ireland. The only way you could have learned of my plans is by talking to the ghost of my father." Liam stopped and looked directly into the man's eyes. "Who are you, Mr. Connolly?" he asked.

"Ah well, now. I see that America has taught you that remarkable trick the Yanks have of coming straight to the point. Over here, Mr. McMahon, we like to let our words dance a little together, get to know each other, like, before they make a commitment."

"Somebody is waiting for me, Mr. Connolly. I don't have time for a courtship."

He turned and began to walk away.

"I know why you're here, Liam."

"Who the hell are you?"

"I'm with the Special Branch. I'm a policeman, Mr. McMahon. A cop. You are here to report on a bank robbery, and a cop might be a very useful fellow to know, don't you think? Especially so since you don't know a soul in Ireland, do you?"

"No. Well, I have a few contacts. Damn. Look, I'm sorry. It's been a long flight."

"It's alright son. Your Da was the same. Never had time to finish a sentence or a pint. Can I drive you to the hotel? It'd give us a chance to talk."

"Sure. Oh, no, I can't. I really do have somebody waiting. A woman from our local affiliate. Perhaps later… this evening, maybe? What are you doing for dinner?"

"Dinner. Yes, I think dinner would be grand. You're staying at the Burlington, aren't you? I'll pick you up about seven. Would that be okay?"

"Fine. What should I wear?"

"Clothes, Mr. McMahon. Clothes. We're a civilized and ancient people, and besides that, it's chilly here on September evenings. Wear some clothes."

Sheila Walsh was arguing with a parking cop outside the main terminal as Liam came out of the building, bags in hand.

"I know he'll be out in a minute, Officer. He's an old man. It takes him a while to get his bearings."

"I'm sorry, Miss, but this is a pick-up area only. You'll have to park in the lot like everybody else."

"I'll have him say a Mass for you. He'll be very grateful if you save him the walk. He's been going all the time since he left Rome, you know."

"Rome?"

"Yes." She looked at the cop's nametag. "The beatification of Saint Kieran. The Monsignor is arguing his case."

"Well . . ."

"Thank you, sir. You're a wonderful man." Liam, laughing, got into the car behind the cop's back. Finding himself in the driver's seat as the Irish drive on the right, he put the car in gear and pulled away from the curb. Sheila jumped in beside him and they took off down the exit ramp, leaving the cop scratching his head.

"Where were you?" she asked, smiling. "Another couple of minutes and I'd have had to produce the Pope himself!"

"Oh," said Liam. "There was a line at the baggage claim."

His room at the Burlington was on the fourth floor. The window faced west, away from the harbor, and overlooked a busy thoroughfare that would have been at home in any major U.S. city.

Liam tossed his suitcase on the spare bed and then gently placed his oversized carry-on bag in the closet. Starting the shower in the adjoining bathroom, he stripped quickly and let the soothing water wash away the stress and fatigue of his journey. Afterward he lay naked on the soft high mattress, shaped a pillow the way he liked it, and within seconds was sound asleep.

At precisely seven o'clock the phone by his bed began to ring. It was the cop, Dick Connolly, and he was waiting in the lobby. Liam dressed hurriedly and took the elevator down to the main floor. Connolly greeted him amiably, ignoring the small delay, and led him outside to a waiting taxi.

The cab merged into the evening traffic that was exiting the city and headed south toward the Wicklow Mountains. Within minutes the landscape changed dramatically. What had been affluent suburbs quickly blended into wild hill country, speckled here and there with a thatched cottage. They passed an ancient abbey and the remains of a feudal tower, and then the car turned right and began to meander deeper into the mountains. Here the slopes were covered with young pine trees, the fruits of a state reforestation program.

A heavy truck passed quickly in the other lane and Liam was startled by its speed and proximity on these narrow curving roads. The cabbie explained that the Irish in general paid little attention to posted speed limits, that breakneck driving was somewhat of a national pastime. As he spoke, he steered his vehicle around a particularly nasty hairpin turn at great speed, all the while looking over his shoulder. Liam was alarmed. He gripped the handle on his door, white knuckled, and then relaxed a little as they came out of the bend. Now the road sloped quickly downward and within a few minutes they entered a quaint village settled peacefully on the valley floor.

"This is Knockmeal" said Connolly. "Your mother's people are from these parts."

Liam looked out the window at the neat rows of white cottages, the tall grey church and the brightly painted shop fronts.

"I know," he said, remembering.

He had spent half of a two-week vacation here when he was fourteen. It had been his mother's idea. Not surprisingly, Liam had a difficult time after the murder. The therapist said a busy schedule would help, but it didn't. By the next summer, Liam's bouts of depression were getting deeper and longer. His sister Joyce, two years older and infinitely more social-minded, was going to a girls' camp in northern Minnesota for the month of August. Moira decided it was time for Liam to meet his family in Ireland, so late that June she booked two round trip tickets for the middle of August.

The taxi rolled to a stop in front of Malone's Pub. Connolly paid the driver and asked him to pick them up at ten. He directed Liam through a small foyer from which two doors led to the two main rooms of the pub. The one to the right was designated as the Bar and Liam could see that it was Spartan in its decor.

"This way," said Connolly as he took Liam's arm and steered him into the Lounge. Here the atmosphere was entirely different. Plush booths lined the walls and wineglass racks ringed the elegant mahogany bar. A tall thin man in a white evening jacket greeted them graciously and asked if they had come for drinks or dining.

"Both!" said Connolly with a laugh, and then pointed to a booth that gave them a commanding view of the whole room, and especially the doorway. Liam wondered if this was a conscious decision, or had Connolly been a cop so long that it was just second nature? The thin man took their drink order and retreated.

On the drive down, they had not discussed anything related to the case because of the cabby's presence. Now Dick Connolly turned in his seat and looked directly at Liam, his grey eyes intense in their gaze. Liam saw intelligence there, but something else, too. Dick Connolly was not a man to cross.

"We had great times, me and your auld fella," Connolly said as the thin man brought the drinks. "We went to school together, you know. Of course, he was always top of the class. I sat in the back with the rest of the omadauns, having a grand old time and getting into trouble. He'd be up front with the swots, eating up the learning.

"We didn't get along too well until we both ended up in University College together, me by the skin of my teeth. We were both from Clare, you see, and there were few enough young people from the West going to Dublin universities in those days. Because we had known each other back home in Ballycoral, we kind of drifted together. We ended up sharing digs on the Rathmines Road and chasing two sisters from Wicklow."

"What were you studying?" asked Liam, intrigued.

"He was taking Irish and mathematics. He was all fired up to become a schoolteacher. Said that was the best way to stay true to his dream. He wanted to educate generations of activists who would one day reunite the country. I read science, mostly. It did me some good later when I joined the police. An interest in forensics eventually got me posted to the Special Branch."

"And the girls . . ." asked Liam.

"Your father chased Moira until she caught him," he said with a smile. "Her sister, your Aunt Beth, was not so lucky. She and I were an item there for a while, but we split up a couple of years later."

Liam sensed that the memory was uncomfortable for Connolly. He took the older man's empty glass to the bar and asked for a refill. When he returned to the table, the cop had recovered his good humor.

"Well," he said. "Enough of this dancing around. Let's talk about why you have come back to us."

"How did you know I was coming?" asked Liam.

"An old friend of mine in Airport security told me. His computer flagged your name because of your father's 'activities' in the old days. He passed the information along to me, knowing of the family connection."

"But how did you know why I was here?"

"Simple," said Connolly. He took a deep drink from his pint of Guinness, wiped the foam off his lips, and looked at the younger man. "I waited until you were in the air and then I called your boss. A fellow called Williams, I believe. He was delighted that the Irish Special Branch were taking an interest in the newspaper's problems, although he spent most of the conversation explaining the need for secrecy. Your Mr. Williams is very afraid of his competition, isn't he?"

"Yes," said Liam, laughing.

A pretty waitress in a black skirt and white shirt approached the booth and took their order. The room was filling up now and the thin man was busy seating well-dressed older couples and groups of prosperous young people. How things have changed here in the past eighteen years, thought Liam.

The last time he had been here, the countryside had been full of subsistence farmers scraping out a living on the rocky hills. Main Street had been empty except on market day. Now it was lined with imported automobiles, not of few of which bore the imprint of a prestigious German manufacturer. Europe had been good to rural Ireland, he thought. Even with the real estate collapse and the big bailout, people were still doing well. How much of the economy was conducted under the table, he wondered?

"What I don't understand" Connolly interrupted his thoughts, "is why your Mr. Williams sent you to Ireland. After all, the break-in took place in London."

"Jerry thinks the codes are here," Liam explained. "The men who killed the London manager were Irish, and one of the ATMs they robbed was in Dublin. Prime's London branch makes all the cards for Irish customers, so the access codes are just as valuable here as in the U.K. Scotland Yard told the Times that there were five gunmen involved in the robbery. Aside from the codes, they also got away with almost twelve million dollars in used notes. We figure they split up after dividing the cash and the leader held onto the codes. We're hoping that he, being Irish, has returned to Ireland, bringing the codes with him."

"What makes you think they split up?"

"So far," Liam said, "bogus cards have been used to rob machines in London, Birmingham, Amsterdam, Boston, and Dublin. In each case only one card was used and only one withdrawal was made. We think they were just testing the system. They could hardly need cash already, considering the twelve million they took."

Connolly nodded. He knew the group were Irish because his counterpart at Scotland Yard had told him that the bank manager's wife had heard them talking. He also knew one other thing that he now shared with Liam.

"Inspector Lowell of the Yard called me this morning," he began. "That bank manager in London was married to a smart woman. Aside from hearing and identifying their accents, she also noted one other thing. The leader, she tells us, was wearing a pair of snakeskin cowboy boots with silver-capped toes."

Liam felt a chill run down his spine.

Sheila Walsh woke slowly the morning after her trip to the airport. Today was Friday and she was immediately cheered by the prospect of the coming weekend. Not that she had any plans yet, but a couple of days away from the office in this glorious September weather was an enticing thought. Actually, she was quite fond of her job. A year ago she had traded in a sure thing as a junior executive with Cashway Bank to become a freelance reporter, and despite the pay cut she was having a ball.

An only child, her father had been a dentist in Athlone, a market town in the middle of Ireland. Her mother was content to stay at home, despite a degree in pharmacology from UCD. Sheila had not understood this until she herself was almost thirty and had lost the urge to become a corporate shark. Several of the women with whom she had graduated were now in prominent positions in large companies throughout Europe, and though she kept in touch with them, she didn't envy their success.

One advantage to being freelance was that, because she was not crucial to the day to day running of the paper, she was always available to do special little jobs like meeting Liam McMahon at the airport. She considered these outings to be perks, although that was hardly the way her editor looked upon them. But a few hours away from the office on company time was a luxury to Sheila and she enjoyed every minute of it.

She hadn't quite figured out why she liked Liam McMahon, but she knew that she did. Perhaps it was the obvious relish with which he enjoyed her little prank with the parking cop, and the short ride to the Burlington Hotel that had been full of animated banter. Sheila had felt very relaxed in his company, and he seemed to be enjoying himself, too.

This morning she was to pick him up at the hotel and bring him to meet Prime Bank's chief security officer at an obscure little office in the suburb of Dundrum. She was quite looking forward to it.

The clerk at the Burlington reception desk wouldn't give her Mr. McMahon's room number, but he was willing to ring the room for her. After he dialed, she took the receiver and waited as the phone rang repeatedly. On the seventh ring she was about to hang up when a hand tapped her gently on the shoulder.

"Looking for me?"

He smiled as she turned around. He was dressed in a light suit and carried the same large tote that he had hauled around the airport the day before.

"Yes," she returned his smile. "All set then?"

"Do you fancy a bite of breakfast?" he asked. A momentary doubt crossed her face as she ran through his schedule in her head.

"Come on," he said, taking her arm gently. "We'll charge it to my publisher."

They made their way to the hotel coffee shop and took a table by the window. His request for hashbrowns, eggs and bacon puzzled the waitress so he asked Sheila to order for him.

"Bring him a big fry," she said to the girl. "Give him rashers and black pudding and lashings of fried bread. Oh, and he's sure to want coffee too, black and percolated. I'll have a croissant and a white coffee, thanks."

Her soft accent charmed him. He was enjoying her company so much he forgot to ask for a translation of the order. However, the food arrived quickly and was delicious. His father had once said that Irish cuisine was excellent, as long as you ordered breakfast three times a day.

As they ate, their conversation was lighthearted and friendly. He was thinking how much more at ease he was in her company that he had ever been with Nancy or any of the other women he dated at home.

"Mind if I join you?" Liam turned to see Connolly standing in the aisle, his hand already reaching for a chair at the end of the table.

"No" said Liam, annoyed at the intrusion but still glad to see the friendly policeman.

"And who might this be?" asked Connolly, his smile directed at Sheila.

"This is Ms. Walsh, another newshound." Liam sensed that Connolly already knew who Sheila was, but he went along with the deception.

"Pleased to meet you, Ms. Walsh. I'm Dick Connolly, an old friend of Mr. McMahon's father."

"Nice to meet you, Mr. Connolly."

"Are you Liam's guide here in Dublin?"

"You might say that. His paper has asked me to look after him while he's in Ireland. I'm doing my best to see he doesn't get lost." And after a brief pause, " Or arrested".

Liam was startled. Had Sheila already guessed Connolly's occupation?

"Do I know you, Ms. Walsh?" the policeman asked calmly.

"No. But I know you. Your face was plastered all over the front page of the Evening Herald about two months ago. Something to do with a jailbreak, wasn't it?"

"You have a good memory, my dear. Yes, it was. I made a right bags of that, didn't I?" He laughed, and then looked at Liam. "I let a fellow get away from me on the way to Kilmainham Jail. He'd just been sentenced in a bank holdup, and I was in charge of transporting him from the courthouse to the jail."

Liam didn't know whether to be more surprised at Connolly's candor or the nature of the assignment. He couldn't imagine any of his hometown cops being so nonchalant in describing a failure. But even more puzzling was the concept of an Inspector with the Special Branch working a routine prison transfer.

"How come you were driving this fellow?" Sheila asked, startling Liam with her forthright approach.

"I see you have picked up Mr. McMahon's habit of asking direct questions." Connolly looked at her for a moment, and then decided to answer.

"This particular gentleman was a known security risk. He has, shall we say, political affiliations."

"You mean he's IRA?" she asked.

"No, not exactly. He was once, but for some time now he has been operating independently. And the boys he used to play with are none too pleased at his antics. I daresay they would be just as happy as ourselves if we could get him back behind bars where he belongs."

"What's his name?" Liam asked.

"Doherty. Fergus Doherty."

"And he's still loose, is he?"

"Unfortunately. The last we heard of him was a sighting in Birmingham."

"Birmingham!" said Liam. "Do you think he's involved in my little problem?"

"Hardly. Mr. Doherty is not that sophisticated. His usual method is to point a shotgun at the first bank teller, shoot him, then move to the next window and make his demands known. He generally gets instantaneous cooperation."

"Why does he sound familiar?" Liam mused.

Connolly paused for a second, wondering if he had already said too much. Then he remembered Liam's father and felt obliged to continue.

"He had a brother once. A long time ago. Mick was his name. You Da knew him well. Anyway, back in '72 the brother died in jail in Belfast, and at the time everyone thought the British had killed him in the course of torturing him."

Liam didn't hear the last few words. Blood rushed to his temples as an image of that horrible night filled his vision. His father and Uncle Seamus. They had been watching the story on the news when the gunmen crashed in. There had been a shootout in Newry. A soldier and three cops had been killed in retaliation for Mick Doherty's murder. Then his father had seen him on the stairs. Uncle Seamus made a joke, and the doors burst open. A man wearing cowboy boots . . .

"Liam, are you okay?"

He opened his eyes to see Sheila Walsh bent over him, genuine concern on her face.

Inspector Connolly decided to accept their invitation to accompany them to the bank's security office in Dundrum. It was in a quaint, turn-of-the-century red brick building that had once been a boarding house. The village's main street meandered past the building and across the street a modern shopping center highlighted Ircland's blend of the ancient and the contemporary. South of the shopping center lay the ruins of a twelfth century castle, and between the two was a stalwart granite Catholic church, its aging spires soaring to the heavens while graffiti blemished its toes.

The security officer was a short, balding man with round metal-framed glasses and a stained tie. His polyester suit and his rotundity combined to induce a constant layer of perspiration on his brow, and his hand when Liam shook it was clammy and cold. His name was Reginald Butler, and Liam took an instant dislike to him.

The bank had learned of the newspaper's interest in the crime, and its Board felt more comfortable managing the information flow than simply ignoring the reporters.

Once the greetings and introductions were out of the way, Butler bade them be seated. He was relishing this opportunity to be the focus of their attention. Acting more as master of ceremonies than host, he asked each one in turn what they knew of the case to date. When it was Liam's turn he hoisted his large carrier bag onto his knee, opened the zipper and pulled out his laptop. He placed the monitor on Butler's desk and let the other three read through his summary of the story to date, while he looked out the window.

Sheila Walsh felt a little out of place. Her function at the Cashway Bank had never been security, and she wondered what her old boss would say if he knew she was being made privy to this information about Prime's problems. However, both Liam and Connolly had accepted her involvement without question, and Butler had obviously not been briefed to exclude her.

When all three had finished reading, Liam asked Butler what he could add.

"Well," the security officer said. "We have only one new development."

"And that is?" asked Connolly.

"It seems" said the fat man pompously, "that one of our gang got greedy. Last night, somebody used a stolen code to access a cash machine in a hotel in Blackrock."

"Where's Blackrock?" Liam asked.

"It's a suburb just south of here, on the Irish sea."

"How much did he take?"

"A couple of hundred pounds. But that's not what is significant here. The card was the same one used in the city center three days ago. Or a copy thereof."

For the first time since leaving Jerry's office, Liam felt optimistic.

The blond man screamed.

Fergus Doherty walked to the window and brushed the grimy curtain aside. The courtyard below was empty. Reassured, he turned his attention back to the scene inside the woodshop. Picking up a roll of plastic packaging tape, he approached his victim. Doherty nodded to his two accomplices and they held their prisoner tight while he taped the man's hand.

Despite the crude bandage, blood dripped from the saw cut where their captive's fingers had just been severed. Doherty danced lithely from its path.

"Did you make any more cards, Jimmy?" he asked.

The prisoner shook his head slowly, his eyes dulled by shock and pain.

"Are you sure?"

A weak nod.

"I must have the truth," said Doherty, reaching for the switch on the table saw.

A deep, distinguished voice spoke from the shadows at the back of the shop. The voice belonged to a tall man dressed in a fine wool suit, his face partly hidden by a large tweed cap.

"Mr. Roach has nothing more to tell you."

The man in wool stepped from the shadows. He stubbed out his long dark cigarette with the toe of a cowboy boot. Then he pulled a silenced Luger from his shoulder holster and with one quick shot delivered the blond man from his agony.

Late that evening, Dick Connolly called Liam at the Burlington where he was dining with Sheila Walsh. The police, working with prime security, had isolated two closed caption images. One was from the city center branch, the other from Blackrock. The same slightly built blond man appeared in both. His name was Jimmy Roach, and he was a longtime acquaintance of Fergus Doherty.

Roach had been picked up for speeding two months ago in Birmingham. Two days prior to that, he had been noticed by Irish immigration officials who had almost detained him as he left Dublin hours after the Kilmainham jailbreak.

Mr. Roach's body had just been discovered in a woodworking shop in north Dublin. Well, most of it had. They were still looking for some fingers.

Early Saturday morning, Sheila picked up Liam at the hotel and they headed out of the city toward County Clare, on the west coast. With everything closed for the weekend, they had decided to visit Liam's father's family on a farm near Loop Head, a finger of land above the Shannon that reached far into the Atlantic and wore a spectacular lighthouse on its crown. A new freeway system delivered them as far as Ennis, and then they took to back roads that meandered through low hills and villages of small, whitewashed homes. As they approached the Atlantic, there were fewer and fewer trees, and none at all within a few miles of the sea.

The farmhouse had been built two hundred years ago on a long graceful slope that descended gently to the cliffs. From a large kitchen window, Liam could see the ocean below and faraway dots of trawlers working their lobster lines. His aunt Sadie was alone in the house: her two sons were on a boat and wouldn't be back until dark. Her husband, Sean, had passed away some years ago.

Sadie plied her visitors with endless cups of tea accompanied by apple tart and sweet biscuits, a huge lunch of boiled potatoes and ham, and then more desserts drowned in fresh, sweet cream. She was delighted with her company and begged for news from home. Her brother, Liam's father, had been a serious scholar all his life, but she still found great stories to tell about his misdeeds as a boy. She kept her guests laughing and eating well into the afternoon, when they finally escaped to walk the cliffs and work off some of the food.

After strolling around the lighthouse and listening to seals bark on the rocks below, they found a spot above the cliffs where generations of visitors had scratched their names in the limestone. Sheila dutifully signed in while Liam watched the boats bob on the waves below. The swell was enormous, much more than the waters of the Pacific along the coast of northern California, where he had vacationed a couple of times over the past few years. Sunlight danced over the water, so bright it almost hurt to watch. A steady breeze pushed up from the sea, blowing Sheila's long hair around her face so that she was constantly fixing it.

He liked watching her.

As they returned to the house, they passed a seemingly abandoned farm tucked into a bend in the road, and Liam was surprised to see a new Audi parked halfway into the tumbledown barn.

The McMahon boys, Dara and Michael, were already home when Liam and Sheila reached his aunt's house. It seems cellphones work on the ocean, and they cut their day a little short to meet their cousin from America and his pretty date from Dublin. They were huge men, rugged and sunburned with massive hands and awkward gaits on land that belied their seafaring ways. Everything about them was oversized, including their humor, and Liam wondered how on earth he could possibly be from the same genes as these gentle giants.

After another huge meal the conversation turned from America to the local area, which Liam had visited for a week as a child. He remembered far more about the nearby village and all of the neighbors who dropped in than his aunt thought he would. The reveries were interrupted when Sheila's phone rang, and it was a call from Inspector Connolly for Liam.

"They caught them," he said. The simplicity of the statement didn't quite register with Liam, and it took him a few seconds to get up to speed.

"Who?"

"Fergus Doherty and three others, all in a car driving onto the ferry in Dun Laoghairc. They were headed back to Birmingham from Dublin."

"You mean, it all over? Just like that?"

"Well, no. Not quite. They still don't know who was behind the whole thing. There's no way Doherty was smart enough to plan this, and the rest of them are just low level thugs who are good with a gun and keep their mouths shut."

"You must be feeling pretty good about getting Doherty back behind bars."

There was a short pause.

"Yes. I suppose a lot of this mess is my fault, isn't it?"

Liam knew the question was rhetorical, and he let it lie. Instead, he talked of the relief they must be feeling in the boardroom at Prime Bank, but Connolly cut him off.

"No," he said. "We got the guys, but we didn't find the codes."

That evening, his aunt showed Liam and Sheila into the guest bedroom where a huge stuffed toy seal lay on a queen-sized bed. Sheila never hesitated. She put her travel bag on a chair in the corner, bounced on the mattress and looked at him with an intimate smile.

In the morning, they again walked the cliffs. On the way back, Liam once more noted the Audi parked in the old barn, and he asked his aunt about it when they got back to the house.

"Oh, that'll be Father Keogh's car," she said. "You might not remember him. I think he was still in America when you were here last. That farm was his father's place."

"I think I remember a Mr. Keogh," Liam said. "He was very old, and used a stick."

"That would have been the Da," Sadie replied. "He has been gone a long time now. Father Keogh and his sister own the farm, and they rent out the land. The roof on the house fell in, oh, maybe ten years back. Come to think of it, there's not much else over there. I wonder why himself would be parked there."

On their afternoon walk, working off a huge breakfast of fried food and a lunch of salad, sandwiches and two desserts, they once again passed the old farm. The car was still there, unmoved. This time Liam's curiosity overcame him, so he walked up to the gate and craned in for a better look. Sheila laughed and said something about only an American having the gall to do something like that. When he opened the gate, she made some excuse about having to visit the bathroom and hightailed it for his aunt's house, laughing loudly as she ran up the road.

Liam walked over to the Audi. Afternoon shadows were beginning to reach into the barn, but he could still see well enough to know that nobody was there.

The house was not as bad as he had thought it would be. Only a small portion of the thatched roof had caved in, and that was over an attached porch. He knocked on the front door and immediately heard a shuffling within. The top half of the door opened and the tousled head of a man about his father's age appeared.

"What is it?" the man asked.

"Oh, I'm sorry to wake you," Liam apologized. "Only, I'm staying at my aunt's down the road and we noticed the car parked in the yard and she said the house was abandoned."

"You're over at Sadie's, are you?"

"Yes. I'm her nephew."

"Liam, is it?" He extended a hand, and Liam shook it, nodding.

"You're the image of your father," the man said, opening the bottom of the door. "I'm Donal Keogh. He and I went to school together. Come on in, son."

"Father Keogh?"

"That's right." He pointed to the wall behind him, where a clerical collar hung on a hook. "And you're back from America, are you?"

"Just for a visit."

"I was there myself for a while. I had a parish in Chicago for a few years in the seventies. Well, it wasn't my parish. But I did enjoy America. Everything is so... young, over there."

"Well, not that young," Liam laughed. "It's been five hundred years since Columbus. And there were a few people there before him, too."

"Five hundred years is a short history," the priest barked. "We had Vikings and Danes and Normans here before your Mr. Columbus ever left his wet-nurse."

Liam was a bit taken aback at the priest's fervent tone. He had noticed before how the Irish were enveloped in their history, but mostly it was a frame of reference rather than belligerence.

"Your father knew his history," the priest continued, as he reached for a kettle and filled it with water. Liam was surprised that the well was still working.

"Yes," Liam agreed.

"And your uncle Seamus, too. They were both good lads."

Something rang a very small bell in Liam's mind. The priest's voice was... familiar. No, not quite that, but he knew that he had heard it before. His aunt said that Father Keogh had been abroad when Liam was in Ireland last, but yet he knew this voice.

"Tea?" the priest asked. He put two cups on the table and a jug of milk between them. "I don't have any sugar."

And now Liam knew.

He looked around the room and, in the corner under a single bed that was shoved against the wall, he saw them.

The origins of "A Terrible Beauty"

William Butler Yeats
by Pirie MacDonald

At daylight on Monday, April 24th, 1916, about 1,600 Irish nationalists took command of several strategic buildings throughout Dublin. Their stated goal was to end five hundred years of British tyranny in Ireland. It took the British Empire a week to subdue the handful of rebels. In the wake of the rebellion, the government executed the leaders and in doing so sparked a national uprising. On January 21st, 1919 the leaders of the movement met in Dublin to form Dáil Éireann, the first independent Irish government, and to adopt a Declaration of Independence. My grand uncle, Michael Colivet, was a member of that first Dail. There followed a war of independence that led to the British suing for peace in 1921, and the subsequent birth of the Irish Republic.

William Butler Yeats, a nationalist at heart and an internationally celebrated poet, wrote about the men and women in the movement, and how their sacrifice had changed a nation...

Easter 1916
William Butler Yeats

I

I have met them at close of day
Coming with vivid faces
From counter or desk among grey
Eighteenth-century houses.
I have passed with a nod of the head
Or polite meaningless words,
Or have lingered awhile and said
Polite meaningless words,
And thought before I had done
Of a mocking tale or a gibe
To please a companion
Around the fire at the club,
Being certain that they and I
But lived where motley is worn:
All changed, changed utterly:
A terrible beauty is born.

II

That woman's days were spent
In ignorant good will,
Her nights in argument
Until her voice grew shrill.
What voice more sweet than hers
When young and beautiful,
She rode to harriers?
This man had kept a school
And rode our winged horse.
This other his helper and friend
Was coming into his force;

He might have won fame in the end,
So sensitive his nature seemed,
So daring and sweet his thought.
This other man I had dreamed
A drunken, vain-glorious lout.
He had done most bitter wrong
To some who are near my heart,
Yet I number him in the song;
He, too, has resigned his part
In the casual comedy;
He, too, has been changed in his turn,
Transformed utterly:
A terrible beauty is born.

III

Hearts with one purpose alone
Through summer and winter, seem
Enchanted to a stone
To trouble the living stream.
The horse that comes from the road,
The rider, the birds that range
From cloud to tumbling cloud,
Minute by minute change.
A shadow of cloud on the stream
Changes minute by minute;
A horse-hoof slides on the brim;
And a horse plashes within it
Where long-legged moor-hens dive
And hens to moor-cocks call.
Minute by minute they live:
The stone's in the midst of all.

IV

Too long a sacrifice
Can make a stone of the heart.
O when may it suffice?
That is heaven's part, our part
To murmur name upon name,
As a mother names her child
When sleep at last has come
On limbs that had run wild.
What is it but nightfall?
No, no, not night but death.
Was it needless death after all?
For England may keep faith
For all that is done and said.
We know their dream; enough
To know they dreamed and are dead.
And what if excess of love
Bewildered them till they died?
I write it out in a verse—
MacDonagh and MacBride
And Connolly and Pearse
Now and in time to be,
Wherever green is worn,
Are changed, changed utterly:
A terrible beauty is born.

~

**To order single copies of this book,
please visit
www.createspace.com/4459250**

**For wholesale orders,
please visit
www.bhsw.org**

~